D1148737

First published in Great Britain in 2011 by Comma Press
www.commapress.co.uk

First published in Istanbul as *Son Tramvay* by Can, 1991.

A CIP catalogue record of this book is available from the British Library.

ISBN    1905583352
ISBN-13    978 1905583355

**LOTTERY FUNDED**

The publisher gratefully acknowledges assistance from the Arts Council England
North West. With the support of the Culture Programme (2007-2013) of the
European Union.

Education and Culture DG

Culture Programme

Culture

This project has been funded with support from the European Commission. This
publication reflects the views only of the author, and the Commission cannot be
held responsible for any use which may be made of the information contained
therein.
This book has been published with the support of the Ministry of Culture and
Tourism of the Republic of Turkey within the framework of the TEDA Project.

Set in Bembo 11/13 by David Eckersall
Printed and bound in England by Short Run Press.

# THE LAST TRAM

by
Nedim Gürsel

Translated by
Ruth Whitehouse

# Contents

# The Last Tram

EVERY NIGHT AS he waits at the stop for the last tram he thinks of the museums he has wandered around, the cafés he has sat in, the street crowds he has mingled with that day, and how the town suddenly becomes deserted. One by one, the lights go out. First in the houses, then in the bars. As the water in the canal darkens, the streets empty. Crowds no longer come out of the station; the constant roar of traffic has stopped. No bicycles are to be seen anywhere. Standing in the neon light of the street lamps, he waits for the tram. Some nights there's an old man nearby, other nights a few workers returning from their shift. Occasionally there's a couple at the stop embracing and kissing on the bench until the tram arrives, their mouths locked in kisses without even pausing for breath. He remembers a woman whose mouth had appealed to him, earlier that evening in the dim light of a shop window. Later, he'd seen that mouth in a hotel mirror, expressing only a desire to get the business over with as soon as possible. Without giving herself to him, she had lain down with him half-dressed, tongue against tongue. He had felt no warmth from her breath on his skin; she had allowed no intimacy, but simply wanted to finish her work as soon as possible.

The tram's lights shine on the canal before it arrives. The yellow light turns a cloudy green as the wheels move along the rails. Before climbing into the last carriage, he looks once more at the canal. His hotel room comes to mind; it's on the top floor, reached by a steep stairway. A bed, wash-basin and dirty walls. A small table in front of the

1

window overlooking the canal. And his papers scattered on the table.

Every night, in the rear carriage of the last tram, as he recalls how he has spent the day, wandering through parks, walking along canals, crossing bridges and eating in cafés, he looks out of the window at brick walls with dark windows framed by open wooden shutters, at stone reliefs on old narrow-fronted buildings. He thinks of the brightness and warmth of life beyond those dark windows where lights are switched on early in the evening, where people sit comfortably in front of their televisions watching the suffering, poverty, torture and injustices of the world. At first he regrets not being one of those people; then he feels glad that he lives alone in this ghostly northern town, with its gritty water, its moneyed people, its light and its greens, ranging from lime to deep olive. He is glad that he has kept his distance from fellow countrymen who speak his language, who have settled here and found work, who have risked every kind of exclusion and contempt, and who have even been beaten up and killed. He needs this loneliness. He needs it, in order to contemplate what he has lost and what he thinks he has lost for ever, to appreciate the closeness he found so suddenly one day with a woman who now lives far away, and to savour the familiar warmth of her words of love in his mother tongue.

The tram makes its way along one of the main roads through the town centre. It passes buildings with strange names which are still unfamiliar and impossible for him to pronounce. Names like *Paleisop de Dam*, *Hoofdpostkantoor* and *Stadsschouwburg*. Then the street narrows; the rails no longer echo in the basement storerooms of old buildings, or in the sitting rooms of houses that each has a hook hanging from its eaves. The earthquake created by those iron wheels does not cause the polished legs of ancient armchairs, the silken lampshades, the seascapes hanging on walls, the Chinese porcelains or the crystal glasses to shudder. He ponders how these objects have been in existence longer than the people, whose wealth had been created through maritime trade and who now live lives of comfort in their waterfront houses. He recalls the pictures he saw at the museum. A white tablecloth and silver plates of oysters: each one soft, tender and transparent, just waiting to be swallowed. A half-peeled lemon on the edge of a plate. The colour is a bit faded, but no matter. Bread sliced with an ivory-handled silver knife, glasses of white wine. And lobsters, each the size of a hand; crabs, fish, flatfish, plump trout and large ocean-going specimens. There is also game. Venison, pheasant and duck. Turkey, chicken, rabbit and birds. Yes, birds. Beautiful speckle-winged birds, from treetops, reed beds and windmills. Silver pitchers of wine, golden plates of fruit. Purple, red and green grapes, each with its individual lustre, freshly gathered strawberries, sea-green apples. Some already bitten, some cut into pieces. Some are round and wet. As if newly plucked from the branch. They are all there for their taste, for the palate. There to be eaten and drunk, sucked and swallowed. But the scattered place-settings, overturned glasses, and abandoned tables remind him of his loneliness. And the hollow-eyed, snub-nosed idiots who were blessed with all these good things. He contemplates how moments of true happiness are so rarely bestowed on mankind in this mortal world; for instance, meeting over a table laden with good food, or lying with a woman in bed; moments of union in the mountains under the blue skies of early summer, or when making passionate love in the waves of the sea. However, he is now a long way from such happiness; he is alone on a night tram. And the yellow tram is passing through the desolate city streets, taking him to his hotel in one of the suburbs. It is taking him to his cramped room, to the loneliness of the light he forgot to switch off. A bit later, if he can conquer his mental fatigue, he will go to his table and try to write some things down. Maybe he will write about his impressions of the city, maybe about the events of a single day. Maybe he will write about the dirty streets where people wander at night after stuffing themselves with delicious fish and wines at their abundant tables in their uncurtained houses, or the skinny girls who sell themselves on the bridge to make money for drugs, or the weariness he shares with the women who sit reading books under red lights in shop windows waiting for customers. In his tiny room, where there is no trace of his country, his past, or even his masochistic sense of being a writer in exile, he will make love with words until morning. Ever since he arrived in this town, this has been the only way he has managed to make love. It is not a fulfilling lifestyle perhaps, but union with a warm, familiar body is a transitory happiness. He will select his words deftly, words that have fallen out of use and ancient words that have never had a use in daily life. Like a blind man feeling his way with a stick, he will try to hear their sounds and touch their realities. Whispering. Will he first hear whispering, or will it be the refrain of a lullaby? Maybe neither. Like a faithful lover, Turkish words will come to him one by one: unconnected, unrelated, individual words. Totally unaware of each other, they will emerge, emerge into the light of day.

The tram proceeds through the dark city streets. It waits a few moments at each stop, though nobody alights or boards. Then it goes over bridges, past fields and through parks. Sometimes the lights of the carriage fall on water, sometimes on pavements. Sometimes on concrete. Stones, trees, flowers are illuminated. Suddenly the light shines on the nakedness of a female statue. A well-proportioned, beautiful body with pert nipples on its marble breasts… The body is beautiful, but indifferent and cold. Like the mannequins in shop windows.

Yes, soon he will make love with words on paper, if he can awaken his memories of former days. Feeling for words bears no resemblance to making love with a marble statue. It requires persuasion and conviction to find, select and retrieve them from the darkness of the past. And then to lovingly caress and combine them, confide in them, merge with them, and experience their sounds, smells and associations. Yet words, like everything else in this city, are not valued for their use, but for their convertibility. When his books are published here - books that are banned in his own country - his Turkish words are transformed into a strange racket of guttural sounds that is accepted without comment. And the translations, formed of continuous rows of semantic clusters the length of this three-carriage tram, of words heaped with vowels and consonants thrown together, are exchanged for red, purple, yellow and brown paper money. He then gives those crisp bank notes, some with long-beaked hazel-eyed birds and others with sharp-nosed, long-haired men in hats, to the women who sit in shop windows at night. A story in his own language is put into a language he does not understand and it then buys him love. One touch per word, one moment of release for a story written painfully at great personal cost. His books, which are carefully printed not on cheap stuff as in his own country but on high quality paper and, according to the translator, published without error, are transformed by means of gaudy toy-like money into women. Beautiful, young, blonde or brunette, alluring women. A look for a sentence, a long leg for two good paragraphs, 'the full works' for a story, or a week of lovemaking for a book. And a complete travesty of his life's work! He smiles to himself. Or rather, the wild child in him that still resists any notion of loneliness or death forces his lips to part. As he attempts to smile, as if trying to drink a bitter, life-saving medicine without pulling a face, he recalls that Turkish woman. She was the first person to really know him, to melt him with her tenderness, to compare the stiff, lonely man by her side to a wild child. When he was with her, a single touch, a single word sufficed at the moment of fulfilment. But now, even if he could form a sentence, a long, really long, well-balanced, polished sentence, he would still not be able to capture the excitement of that one word, their closeness at the climax of boundless pleasure, the frenzied enthusiasm of making love in the same language. Everything is now so distant, so inaccessible.

He once tried to explain that feeling. It was at a meeting of Turkish writers living abroad; most of them had escaped the fury of martial law and sought refuge in European countries. The city council had organised the meeting in the name of democracy and freedom of thought, and as an opportunity to combat homesickness. Right from the start, he and any other writers who shared his sensitivities were subjected to brutal attacks and criticism by writers who saw themselves as socialists. How else was the country to be saved? Who else, other than they, would save their ravaged country from its black fate? The writer on the podium ranted on about people like Namik Kemal, the Young Turks and Nazim Hikmet, shouting that in times of oppression it was the writer's duty to save his country and lead the people to freedom. The speech finished with the words, "Colleagues, let's extinguish this inferno together!" He had responded without feeling any need to defend himself because, like most of the people there, he was still under investigation in Turkey, where his books were banned and he had been taken to court several times. He had explained that there was no reason for any feelings of pride or heroism, and that writing and fire-fighting were two separate activities that should not be confused. Immediately, all hell broke loose of course. The hall was full of serious, bushy-moustached, mainly 'rustic' writers who shunned him on the pretext that he had *petit bourgeois* values, individualist or pornographic leanings, or even that he was a pervert. At the end of the meeting, all the writers, who in no way resembled fire-fighters, had gone off to the shop windows to quash the raging fires within them.

'Those people,' he mutters to himself. 'They could never be fire-fighters. In old Istanbul, it was an honour to be a fire-fighter, a way of life and something to be proud of!' As he remembers old Istanbul, he recalls a red tram. An old tram creaking along from Sishane to Beyoglu. He and his father are sitting just behind the purple-tinted glass separating the driver from the passengers. He is looking out of the window; his father is looking at him. He is so proud that his son has passed the entrance exam to Galatasaray Lyçee. Soon, he will register him at that famous school, Mekteb-i Sultani![1] They will alight at the Galatasaray stop and walk under the pine trees at the school entrance. As they bid farewell, his father will urge him to be good until he sees him again at the end of the week. Now he sits next to his father, right at the front, and looks out as the tram trundles towards Istiklal Caddesi. He feels strange inside. His sorrow at leaving home for the first time is mixed with excitement at starting a new life at boarding school. As the tram makes its way past the shop windows of Istiklal Caddesi, he sees cakes, toys, books and clothes illuminated in a colourful array of lights, as if at a funfair. As yet, he has no idea that there can be even larger shops that display women for sale. Or that three days later, while he is peacefully asleep in the dormitory, his father is to die in a traffic accident. Nor does he know that trams will be abolished that very year. Within a few months the rails will be torn up and the trams replaced by large, clumsy, trolleybuses with rubber tyres. A story lasting a hundred years, from horse-drawn trams to those 'dangerous and illegal' electric trams, came to an end at the same time as his father's life, which spanned less than half a century. That day, he made his last tram journey in Istanbul with his father. Years later, he boards the last tram in this northern town and, not realising that each stop takes him further away from his past, savours the happiness of watching the world through a tram window.

1. The Sultan's School.

# The Handkerchief

With their milk-white wings fluttering above the murky stagnant water of the canal, the gulls look flawless in the spring sunshine as they fly back and forth: from the green-painted steel girders of the bridge at Pantin, to the roofs of some old peeling stucco buildings and on to the trees visible through a maze of television aerials, and from the sprouting branches of the trees along the canal to my window. However, the silence of my room, which looks out at an overcast wintry sky, is no longer filled with the sense of distant yearning created by Madame Suslova's tired old fingers flitting from key to key with the lightness of a gull, sending notes flying into the inner courtyard and up its depressingly high walls towards my kitchen window. There is no Chopin to transport me, to soothe the fire raging inside me. It is spring and Madame Suslova is no longer here.

Barges, starting out at jetties on the banks of the Seine or at large ports humming with giant cranes exposed to ocean winds, glide through the muddy water of the river from one end of Paris to the other, threading between its broad boulevards and narrow streets and squeezing beneath ancient stone bridges to arrive here in front of my window. They empty their loads at the jetty of the flourmill. The washing hanging on their decks gleams white in the spring sunshine. The holds in their enormous bellies are loaded with sand or wheat. Pigeons dart out of broken factory windows to attack the jetty. They not only pick at the wheat spilling from the sacks, but at my brain as well. They peck away, devouring the past, the beautiful days, everything. I have to put up with this, as well as Madame Suslova's absence. The factories, with their chimneys and brick walls as high as skyscrapers, delve deep into the past. *Les Grands Moulins de Pantin*[2] grind away time with their heavy millstones.

From my window, I see trees along the side of the canal and a few new sugar-pink houses, incongruous in their surroundings. And cosy lives behind undrawn curtains. Well-furnished sitting rooms, pleasant kitchens, children's rooms. In the cool of the evening, the canal traffic is augmented by elderly folk walking their dogs and children running about and playing. One after another, gulls and barges go back and forth along water murky with years of sediment. Before she caught cold and took to her bed, Madam Suslova used to dress Zoe up, put on her collar and take her out for an evening stroll if it was dry. It has hardly stopped raining this year, so whenever I saw them walking by the canal, a strange optimism stirred inside me as I watched Madam Suslova's patient but tired attempts to keep time with Zoe's tiny steps.

Spring was almost upon us. The snowy nights and short dark days were left behind; the cold spell was broken. While Madame Suslova was at the end of her life, I was in the middle of mine. But we were both halfway towards a turning point. We were bound to return to our countries one day. She to the waterways of her childhood in St Petersburg, I to Istanbul and the days of my youth spent on the shores of the Golden Horn. If only spring had come; if only the earth had become warm, the canal water clean. If only the sun had shown its face between the clouds scattered across the wintry skies and restored the colours of the houses and walls.

Well, spring came, even to this remote suburb of Paris, on the flawless milk-white wings of the gulls. Washing dried on the decks of the barges. Dog-walkers were to be seen going up and down the canal. They looked so joyful and happy, almost ready to join in the energetic games of the

2. Iconic Parisian flourmills.

children. But you were not with them, Madame Suslova. My dear, lovely neighbour, Anushka. Why did you have to die, leaving me here alone in the silence of my room, which no longer resounds with melodies from your piano? Why, for the love of God, why did you have to die before spring came? Was it because of the handkerchief you left in my room on that snowy night?

Of course it was not without reason that I had left my room in central Paris and moved out to Pantin. I had liked my room there, even though there was no kitchen and the toilet was at the end of a long dark corridor. I had seen much worse. Rooms with only a skylight, others with no running water, or so small there was no space to move once a bed and table were in there, or rooms of geometrically awkward shapes… My room there was a bit different from the usual Paris attic room. It was larger, there was a lift and it was extremely pleasant, even if the walls were a bit dirty. It was enough for me. I was living alone and had no money. I was expecting to return to Istanbul as soon as martial law was lifted. However, winter struck and snow collected on the roof, where it froze. The temperature went down to minus fifteen. I waited in vain for the weather to warm up again, for ocean winds to drive in clouds bringing rain instead of snow. After the roofs, everywhere else was covered with snow, even the traffic-laden main streets. There was no way of keeping my room warm. In the end, I was forced to move here, with the help of a friend, into this centrally-heated studio apartment on the fourth floor of an old building overlooking the canal. As soon as I moved in, I found a note signed by Madame Suslova in my letterbox. 'From your name you are obviously Turkish. Please come to tea one day and we'll talk about Istanbul.'

Fearing that my loneliness in Paris would become even more intense in this suburb, I wanted to meet my new neighbour on the top floor straight away. When I rang the bell, she greeted me somewhat aloofly. She was wearing a

11

black outfit that was too big for her small frame. Her white hair was tied back in a bun, and she had deep wrinkles on her forehead. With her withdrawn look, dark blue eyes and thin lips, she looked like the women you see in old photographs. There was a strange sorrow, a remote melancholy about her. She looked older and unhappier than she actually was. This was perhaps partly because I was comparing her with the single women I was familiar with in Chekov's plays. However, as soon as we got over our initial shyness, we warmed to each other. She too had recently moved here. She made a living out of giving piano lessons. In a way, it was the relentless winter that brought us together and turned us so quickly from mere neighbours into friends with a common destiny. The weather was so cold, and there was so much snow that we could not go out anywhere, so we kept visiting each other. She usually invited me for tea and, after regaling me with stories of little Zoe's adventures, she would be on the point of talking about her life and her past, and about the time she spent in Istanbul during her youth, but then would stop and go over to the piano, saying, 'Let me play something to you before you go.'

Madame Suslova was extremely sensitive and reserved, and perhaps too proud. Now that I think about it, I never once heard this aristocratic woman complain. This woman, who had been forced to leave her country after the October revolution, led a simple life in her studio with just a grand piano, two armchairs and a single bed, making do with pleasures of the intellect and brief moments of happiness. Yet who knows what she had experienced, what she had seen and lived through? What had she felt when she was leaving Leningrad, which she still called St Petersburg? Why had her father used up all the family's money in the gambling dens of occupied Istanbul? When they migrated to Paris, why had she dropped out of the conservatoire and gone to work on the shop floor of a big department store? As the years passed and she lost relatives and friends one by one, why did she never for a moment lose hope that she would return home? I will never know the answers to these questions. In fact, Madame Suslova said very little and told me almost nothing about her life. But she played the piano all the time. She spoke with the language of Chopin, Tchaikovsky and Mozart. It was through Chopin's nocturnes, mazurkas and his preludes, sorrowful as memories and soft as snow, that she expressed her pain at being uprooted and in exile and her secret desire to be suddenly swooped up and carried away.

That was why I didn't resort to the dreadful writer's habit of creating an embellished life story for Madame Suslova. Sometimes I thought about her in Istanbul, left with her mother in an old house while her father went out to womanise and clink glasses with the war-rich in the restaurants of Pera. I had to imagine how, thanks to her mother, the piano lessons she had started in St Petersburg were continued in Istanbul and how, even when things became really bad after arriving in Paris, she had not given up the piano. Every time I listened to Madame Suslova spilling out her adventures and secrets, not with words but with her fingers, I understood her a little more.

I would listen to Madame Suslova in the evenings, sitting by the piano sipping tea brewed in the samovar, or in the mornings as I tried to write at my table in the frozen grey light of winter. The snow fell continuously. Even a blue-eyed blonde girl in St Petersburg would have feared to look out of the window at the darkness of the frozen canal. The storm of a scherzo with frenzied chords would suddenly subside and the lamp-lit room would be soothed by the sound of a lullaby her mother used to sing. Apart from the fact that she was no longer surrounded by the velvet armchairs and gilded dining chairs, the piano and sideboard with its array of unwanted vases, the pictures on the wall, that little girl would scarcely have realised she was in a different world, with different people and different canals, far from the clutter of those familiar things. She would drift into fantasies and the sweet embrace of sleep. Her fingers would fly up and down the keyboard, which shuddered as if from an earthquake, and the eighth prelude would shower snowflakes, not over city roofs but the sorrowful hearts beneath.

The little girl would be forced to leave her home and everything she loved and, years later, would look out of a different window at the murky waters of another canal. For her, the days she spent away from her country would be like this still, turbid and muddied water. Days of exile, when the sediment that had sunk to the bottom drew her into loneliness and depths of yearning. The little girl's hands, soft as cotton wool on the keyboard, would become the bony, veined, wrinkled hands of an old woman who had not tasted pleasure. As they caressed the keys, her outstretched fingers were tender and merciless, angry and passionate. And so, as Madame Suslova played Chopin upstairs and I wrote at my desk, as the lamps lit up the canal on snowy nights, illuminating a past of long ago, childish rhymes and fairy-tales would come to an end, and the little St Petersburg girl would hug her dolls and go back to sleep.

One night, I was just getting ready to go to bed when there was a knock at the door.

'Who's there?' I called.

'It's me,' replied Madame Suslova in a low voice. 'I need to talk to you.' I opened the door. She entered, with a gush of cold air. She perched on a chair and, with sorrowful, tired eyes, looked around.

'I'm disturbing you, I know, but I need to talk to you.'

'You're not disturbing me. We haven't seen each other for a while. Tell me, what's the news?'

'Nothing. Everything's the same as usual.'

'How is Zoe?'

'She hasn't been too good recently, like me.' She pulled a white, lace-edged handkerchief out of the pocket of her faded and worn black skirt and blew her nose a few times.

Then she apologised, explaining that she had caught a cold while out shopping and now had a fever. She did not look at all well. There was a long silence.

'You know,' she said, 'I've always wanted to talk to you about Istanbul. I wanted you to know that in fact I both lived and died there.'

This was something I could understand. She had met her first and only love in Istanbul; it was in Istanbul that her young heart had begun to flutter. And then... Well, we know what happened then. She was abandoned to sorrow and poverty, her dreams shattered. Seeking happiness through the piano.

'Were you a piano teacher?' I asked.

She expressed no surprise. It was as if she thought I would ask her that question, as if she thought I knew every last detail of her life.

'Yes. I was twenty. He was also Russian, a count.'

I thought of Istanbul during the years of the armistice. The armoured units at the entrance to the Bosphorus, the famous balls held in the mansions of Bebek, Tarabya and Büyükdere, the waltzes to the melody of 'The Blue Danube', the revolving chandeliers and mirrors, the twirling earrings and epaulets, the bubbling champagne flowing like water, the roulette wheels driving so many lives into whirlpools of despair. Did they first meet at Pera Palace? Or at the cloakroom attendant's booth? No, Madame Suslova had first seen her count in the Petrograd Café on Cadde-i Kebir. It was his monocle and abundant beard, and the cane and gloves he placed on the table, that had attracted her attention. He was wearing a frock coat and trousers designed in Paris by Paul Poiret, with a cravat tied outside his stiffly-starched collar. The spats on his shoes were a bit muddy. He was looking at the crowds in the street, the passing horse-drawn trams and perilous phaetons, listening to the hum of the dark stone buildings opposite, which looked as if they were about to come tumbling down on top of the fat Russian woman sitting in the cash booth. When he boarded the ship at Odessa, the same hum had been in his ears – that disturbing, indefinable hum of people with no future. As if the wind was howling in the beech woods of Neva, and melting ice was making the water flow. Soon there would be nobody left in Nevsky Prospect, and the *Aurora*[3] would bombard the Winter Palace. He turned his gaze away from the people in the street and looked inside, where he saw a mother and daughter sitting at the farthest table; he got up and, leaning on his cane, went over to them. It was not the count's sparkling black eyes that had remained in Madame Suslova's memory ever since, but the elegance with which he had kissed her mother's hand. They had left the café together and gone to a concert on the top floor of the Pascal Keller department store in Hacopulo Passage. As the chamber music played, she had been unable to take her eyes off the count. The cello exuded a rich cascade of calm, and the violins shimmered delicately in the air at each entry. After the concert, her mother had replied with a meaningful smile to the count's suggestion about piano lessons, while Anushka had tried hard to hide her excitement. The piano lessons started, followed by secret meetings, the first declaration, the first kiss, walks in the sunset and promises, promises… The dream ended and her world came crashing down when the count squandered all her money at the Cercle d'Orient roulette table and married a rich widow. Now, when Madame Suslova played the piano, the sorrows of the past, the tears for an extinct love, sank deep into the sediment of the Golden Horn and the canals of St Petersburg.

'He was my piano teacher,' she repeated. 'I learned everything from him. Chopin, Tchaikovsky, even how to kiss.'

Feeling she had said too much, she fell silent. In the

3. Russian cruiser. A shot from her forecastle gun signalled the beginning of the assault on the Winter Palace, Saint Petersburg; a pivotal act in the October Revolution.

twilight, I saw her pale face blush slightly. She said nothing more. Like an adolescent girl, she spent the whole evening with her nose upturned. I brewed some tea for her. Then I talked about Istanbul, my Istanbul. The narrow, muddy streets of Kasimpasa, the timber houses and mosque courtyards. The golden vodkas served by waitresses, compatriots, at the Rejans Restaurant and that first rapturous fire in my guts, a fire that has never been dowsed. I spoke of the dark corridors at my boarding school, of the naked women who entered my dreams at night, of the blue light in the dormitory. Of that blinding light that still haunts me and interrupts my sleep. As always when listening to me, Madame Suslova was looking out of the window, not at me. She had fixed her eyes on some distant point beyond the window. Then the snow started. We watched the snow falling together. The buildings opposite disappeared from view. One by one, the lights shining on the canal were extinguished. After a while, Madame Suslova said she had to leave. I showed her to the door. When I returned to my room, I saw a used handkerchief on the floor. It belonged to Madame Suslova. Picking it up, I quickly ran up the stairs and knocked at the door. She opened it immediately. At first she was surprised to see me there.

'I think you forgot this.'

She looked completely bewildered. Her lips began to tremble. 'For Heaven's sake,' she managed to whisper, avoiding my eyes. 'I would never have expected such an insult from you.'

I could not think what had made me go there. She was right. Why was I in such a hurry to return this grotty handkerchief to its owner? Why, in a single moment, had I sullied everything between Madame Suslova and myself? Without allowing me to offer an apology, she shut the door in my face. We never spoke again. She did not reply to the notes and letters of apology I left in her letterbox. Just once, we passed on the stairs, but she ignored my greeting.

Everything would have been fine if only she had just listened to me and forgotten about my error; our friendship would have continued to grow stronger than ever. But it did not happen. Madame Suslova's heart had been broken. When a young girl's heart is broken, it can never be repaired, whatever you do. Inside that old, wrinkled body, Madame Suslova still carried the heart of a young girl. A girl's broken heart which, ever since it first fluttered with the excitement of love in Istanbul, my beloved city, had lost none of its freshness or childishness. That time we passed on the stairs was the last time I saw her. One week later, as the snows began to melt, she died. Nobody attended her funeral except for a few students and me. The porter took Zoe in and her piano was donated to an orphanage. The keys touched by Madame Suslova are now touched by some little girl's fingers, soft and white as cotton wool. Now it is spring.

# Weird Mustafa

THEY HAD FINALLY arrived. Before they went to settle into the cramped rooms allocated to them at a hostel in one of the city suburbs, they had been squatting in a corner of the station, away from the crowds, with their wooden trunks, bulging nylon bags and sorrowful looks. Without talking or complaining, without any mention of the waterways they had seen from the train window during their journey, the spotlessly clean villages with their plump cattle, the fields ploughed by tractors, the overcast autumn skies above distant fields, the shadows on the water from the trees that sped past the windows, or the cathedrals and crowded stations, they lit their cigarettes with a strange feeling that, after traveling for days and nights, they had arrived in their own country, their own village, rather than a busy city in a foreign land, a different world. They inhaled their cigarettes next to trains that had come from the four corners of the Earth, near enormous clocks and information boards that turned automatically to show the names of towns, platform numbers and details of delays. They walked without intermingling with the beautiful blonde women, the businessmen looking refreshed and smug at having made the first train of the morning, or the uniformed officials wandering about with their pompous air. Holding nervously on to the escalator handrail, they went down into the underground in small groups.

Never mind how they lost their way in the Métro, how they clung to each other in the city turmoil, how they were afraid of the automatic glass doors and the movement of traffic prompted by lights that turned from red to yellow, from yellow to green and then to red again, or how they were dumped like startled birds or gullible children in a world that was merciless, or rather, indifferent, towards them. No, I shall follow just one of them - Mustafa. In fact, there is a story to tell about anyone who sets foot in a foreign country after a long journey and seeks directions without knowing the language. This is especially so if they are from a village on the Anatolian plain, if they have been plucked from their one piece of land and the shade of a nearby poplar tree and thrown into the middle of Europe's most famous, most striking and most depraved city.

Of course, Mustafa's tale is not about his hands, calloused from years of ploughing, his puny body, his over-sized polished shoes, or the decayed teeth that show when he smiles. This story has nothing to do with his village or the social environment from which he came. And it also has nothing to do with the long hazardous walk from the Gare de Lyon to a single room at a migrant workers' hostel in a northern suburb of Paris. Others can write about Mustafa's adventures in Paris, about how the French sneered at him and exploited him at the factory where he worked, and what he had to put up with in order to get a residence permit. These have been written about already; there is even a literary genre called "migrant workers' literature" which focuses on their social problems. The bitter sweet incidents that happen to Turks in European cities where they form the largest ethnic minority - in France, Germany or even Holland and Sweden - have been written about endlessly. I shall write about Mustafa's obsession, a story of unrequited love. To do this, it is not enough merely to trace our hero as he goes about his daily life, or to seek a solution to his problems. I need to get inside his head and feel his heartbeat. Yes, his heartbeat...

Mustafa first felt his heartbeat quicken at noon on a

summer's day. He'd just returned from the army and was working in the fields. The August sun was more scorching than ever, a treacherous golden orb in a blue sky. He put down his sickle and wiped his brow with his sleeve. When he stopped, the rustle of wheat stopped too. Then he emptied a jug of water over his head. That cooled him down a little. But before long, he felt the sun beating down on him even more strongly, right into his brain. His whole body was burning furiously; he felt as if he was being roasted alive. Like a red-hot poker, the sun seemed to be piercing his brain and twisting in his head, making sparks fly out of his eyes. The ears of wheat suddenly seemed to melt to nothing in the heat. Mustafa tottered towards a poplar tree where he threw himself down in the shade. He lay there on his back, looking up at the sky through the leaves. Somehow the sky seemed much bluer and the sun less scorching. And the earth was cooler, friendlier. He does not remember what happened next. All he knows is that his heart began to beat in time to the rustle of the leaves. The poplar seemed to be whispering in his ear, whispering the first words of love he had ever heard:

'Are you tired, my lion? My brave young man. My one and only. Like tears, I shed my leaves for you!'

Nobody, not even his mother, had spoken to him so gently, so lovingly, until that day. The lullabies he'd heard as a child, the songs they chanted in the army - none of them had affected him as deeply as the words of the poplar. Mustafa wasn't surprised, even though he knew that trees were not supposed to speak. Didn't cockerels and foxes, giants and dwarves, fairies and witches talk in the stories his grandmother used to tell him? The owls that hooted in the forest, the stones that rolled down the hillside, the clouds that rained, and the blind grandmother's cane - they all talked, so why not a poplar that showered bright green leaves on his head like sparkling water? He submitted himself to the magical voice of the tree.

'Come to me, my Mustafa! Be my fire, my heart's desire, let me soothe you when you tire,' the poplar was saying. 'I watch you as you reap the corn, without you I was so forlorn. Your eyes so dark, your head so straight, to rest here with me is your fate. My roots will embrace you, my leaves caress you. My shade will envelop you with love.'

How beautiful the poplar's words were. How cool its shade, how its leaves rustled and trembled. For the first time, Mustafa felt a thrill of pleasure and was transported into a state of ecstasy. That poplar remained with him always. He used to speak to the poplar and the poplar spoke back. They confided in each other, told each other their problems, and finally they became star-crossed lovers. There was a saying that, 'Trees are devoured by worms, people by problems.' Mustafa's problem was the poplar, and the poplar's worm was Mustafa, but they got by without upsetting each other.

However, their happiness did not last long. One day, Mustafa, who was not surprised at finding happiness with the poplar, was startled when his father said, 'It's time you got married.'

He didn't know what to say. They asked for the hand of a girl in a neighbouring village and her family asked Mustafa's family for the dowry. And his father, who had said to Mustafa, 'I planted this poplar, you make it grow,' went and chopped the poplar down to raise money for the dowry. The tree fell as if struck by lightning, but there was no sound from Mustafa.

He did not cry out, like most lovers, 'Woe is me!' He didn't say, 'Please, don't do it! It's wrong!' He just went off silently, his head bowed. As time passed, the hope that had taken root inside him and the passion that had inflamed his heart were extinguished. He spoke to no one, never set foot outside the house. But the night before his wedding, he went out and never came back.

Now, Mustafa has returned from work to his room in a northern suburb of Paris; he bolts down some food and goes straight to bed. In his dream he sees a beautifully slender, graceful poplar with leaves rustling in the wind on the plain. The poplar is talking to Mustafa in that soft feminine voice:

'Oh my lion, my hero! Bravo! Thank God you didn't slay me. You got your own back on that lowlife father of yours. You took revenge on my behalf and have given your heart to no other!'

Mustafa smiles in his sleep. Sometimes he sees his beloved mother in his dreams.

'You left and never came back,' she says.

'Yes… I left and never came back…'

'…'

'So, did the frost get to them?'

'To the crops?'

'No, not the crops, the poplars.'

'No, this year the winter left early, like you.'

In his sleep, Mustafa smiles happily because the frost has not blighted the poplars. Then he asks for news of his village. Because the flocks of flamingos that manage to fly over mountains and plains are unable to scale the concrete skyscrapers and reach the television aerials. They can't get up there to give Mustafa news about his village.

'Ali, Rustem the wrestler, Hasan? How are they all?

'Oh, you know. Same as always. The wrestler went to jail this year - crime of honour. Hasan got himself shot near the spring. Poor kid, it was a shame. You used to like him, didn't you?'

'Who did it?'

'…'

'Who did that to Hasan?'

'Who knows? Some twisted guy. They say Halil Aga had him shot.'

'Halil! I hope he rots in Hell!'

'Steady! Someone might hear!'

'…'

'God bless his family.'

'Yes, God bless them.'

Suddenly, Mustafa flushes. He wants to ask, 'Did they plant a new poplar tree?' But though the words are on the tip of his tongue, he cannot utter them. He cannot ask the question.

His mother complains, 'You can't abandon a bride on her wedding night. Shame on you!' Mustafa says nothing. He feels a poplar tree toppling inside him, a green poplar with its roots in water and its branches in the clouds.

On Sundays, Mustafa wanders the streets alone. Everywhere's closed, everyone's at home. He walks past doors, windows and walls. Whenever he finds a café open, he goes and sits inside for a while. Then he goes back out into the suburban asphalt streets with their concrete walls. There's no park to sit in, not even a patch of green. And no poplar trees. Towards evening, as the sun sets, after walking for miles along side streets and high roads, across empty squares, he reaches the canal. He squats under one of the poplar trees by the edge of the murky water. But when he raises his head to look up through the leaves, he can't see the sky. The sky grew dark long ago. The earth smells strange. The poplar doesn't rustle in the wind, doesn't speak to him. It doesn't say a word. It doesn't whisper a single word of love to create a flicker of passion inside him. *This country's poplars are as strange as its people*, thinks Mustafa. *You'd never marry one of them.* Then he gets up and walks along by the canal. A barge passes, clean washing drying on the deck. He walks on, keeping up with the barge. He needs a woman now. A woman to do his washing and mend his clothes. But he immediately dismisses the idea from his mind. Because wherever he looks and whoever he speaks to, he feels abandonment and alienation inside. He sees the same loneliness on cinema billboards, in shops, in the steamed-up windows of crowded cafes, and on the made-up faces of women sitting opposite him on the Métro. As if the people of this city are receding further and further away from him.

Concrete walls, houses and cafés. And poplars. Still, silent poplars all along the canal on Sundays. Everything and everyone recedes, leaving behind only a painful vacuum. A vacuum that in Mustafa's mind is shrouded by the plains of his homeland. Smooth and formidable. Silently, it envelops the falling poplar trees. The leaves do not stir, yet one after the other the poplars fall. He smiles, thinking how one day he will plant a poplar here in this foreign soil; he will water it, care for it with his own hands and fall in love again. That is why Mustafa keeps smiling, whether it's appropriate or not, whether he's asleep or awake. And when he smiles, he shows his decaying teeth. The premature wrinkles on his face become deeper. The plain leaves its mark on a man for ever. The treacherous summer sun of foreign lands is brutal, especially if you leave your country because of love. And weird Mustafa's beloved is still a brightly adorned poplar tree.

# In the Islamic Cemetery

'DEATH IS IMPARTIAL-'[4] said an ancient Persian poet. The train interrupts the verse right in the middle, as if cutting it with a knife. The damp earth shakes with the thundering of its wheels. For a moment the ground seems to slip from beneath my feet. I think all hell is breaking loose. Everything is turned upside down, as if the Promised Day has arrived, when not a stone will remain standing: the edifices of depravity will come tumbling down and the city of Paris will collapse and disappear.

A voice suddenly spouts words I have not heard for years: long-forgotten, ever-fearsome words, that rained down on the congregation from the mosque pulpit, like flames from the mouth of a fire-eating acrobat:

'Believers! Oh ye who live in fear of the wrath of God, my Muslim brothers! The Al-Zalzala chapter of the Holy Koran tells us: When Earth is shaken with her final earthquake, and the Earth brings forth her burdens, and man saith: What aileth her? That day she will relate her chronicles, That day mankind will issue forth in scattered groups to be shown their deeds.[5]

'And in the Al-Qari'a chapter, received in Mecca, the great God says: "The terrible calamity! What is the terrible calamity? And what will make you comprehend what the terrible calamity is? The day on which men shall be as scattered moths, And the mountains will become as carded wool. But he whose balance of good deeds will be found

4. From *Ölüme dair* [About Death] by Nazim Hikmet.
5. *The Holy Qur'aan* (trans M Pickthall)

light, will have his home in a bottomless pit. His abode shall be the abyss. And what will explain to thee what this is? Raging Fire.'"[6]

'Come on, let's go now, Grandfather. I'm frightened, really frightened. We've performed our rituals, said our prayers. Why are we still standing here?' *Oh God, forgive my sins. Protect this poor little slave from the torments and suffering of hell! May God's angels look down on me favourably!*

And the voice was preaching about the Day of Judgment, when the sun and the moon will come together, the skies will melt like metal, and the mountains will move and come crashing down on the blushing faces of sinners.

'And God says: And on the day when the trumpet shall be blown, then those who are in the heavens and those who are in the Earth shall be terrified except such as Allah please, and all shall come to him abased. And you see the mountains, you think them to be solid, and they shall pass away as the passing away of the cloud – the handiwork of Allah Who has made every thing thoroughly; surely He is aware of what you do.'

Is it only clouds that pass away? Years too have passed away. Gone, like the train that shook the earth. I saw it gliding along dazzling rails in a beautiful light after the rain. It was taking travellers, reclining in their comfortable seats, to the cold, misty cities of the north. Perhaps it was the Amsterdam express that went past, perhaps the Hamburg mail train. Or perhaps it was only going as far as Brussels. It will stay there overnight and bring back different passengers the following morning, still with the same thundering noise, the same speed. At any rate, the Gare du Nord in Paris is the last stop, the last resting place.

'Death…' I repeat. 'Death is impartial… said an ancient Persian poet.' *O God, I can't for the life of me remember the next line! The first is okay, but the next one…* I must have lost the piece of paper my mother pressed into my hand in Istanbul.

6. 'Al-Qaria' [The Calamity], *The Holy Qur'aan*, ibid.

The train obviously cut off my memory as well as the poem. My mind was befuddled by the dazzle of the wet rails. Maybe it wasn't the earth that shook, but my faith. That's right, it wasn't my belief that the future promised to be as good as the present that was shaken, but my belief in the Unity of God and the Day of Judgement. The train carried me away from the small town of my Muslim childhood, from the domination of the imam, with his fiery voice and fearful teachings, and brought me here to this strange place in a northern suburb of Paris. It brought me here and left me, like an incongruous seed in soil watered by the rain, or like an alien object left on a beach by the sea.

The earth smells of rotting leaves. But cypress trees don't shed their leaves. They stand rustling over gravestones, flat or upright, large or small. I'm in the Islamic cemetery at Bobigny. To the left are a few slender cypresses along the railway; opposite is a factory's scrap metal depot. The walls of the cemetery are so low that the inside of the depot is visible from where I'm standing. Beyond the walls there are two-storey houses, electricity cables and, in the distance, the TDF tower and the skyscrapers that surround the city. Like a giant equipped with the most advanced instruments of modern technology, the tower seems to challenge the city. It dominates everything. It monitors us with its face turned towards the city and the cemetery. Me and the imam.

'Everyone will taste death,' says the imam, in a weary voice, as we walk along, side by side. 'Let's stop here and recite a Fatiha[7] for the souls of the dead. Because according to the Koran, our Holy Prophet was instructed that the seven Ayas of Al-Fatiha were given to be repeated over and over again.' I feel as if I'm in Anatolia, in the provincial town of my childhood, rather than Bobigny. As if I'm going through the market to perform *namaz*[8] with my grandfather at the mosque.

7. First chapter of the Koran.
8. Formal prayer.

'My boy,' said my grandfather, 'you're still young, but there are things you should know. After performing *namaz*, we must recite a Fatiha for the dear souls of our dead, our martyrs and the great Atatürk, saviour of our country. So, start reciting. Let me hear you.'

At first I hesitated. Then my memory started to work rapidly. In a single breath, without understanding, I recited the words of the Fatiha, one after the other, right to the end.

'Hey, you forgot "In the name of Allah,"' said Grandfather. 'You have to say "In the name of Allah" at the start of every prayer!' I started again without any sign of irritation. Stubbornly and fervently, I recited the Fatiha from beginning to end in one breath, this time putting "In the name of Allah" at the beginning,

'Good boy. Very good,' said Grandfather in a pleased voice. 'But you forgot to say "Amen" this time. At the end of every prayer, you must say "Amen"!'

I started the Fatiha for the third time: 'In the name of God, the Lord of Mercy, the Giver of Mercy! Praise belongs to God...' I couldn't remember any more! How hopeless I felt among the crowds in the market! I clasped my grandfather's hand in fear. He seemed to be pretending he was not my grandfather, as if he'd disowned me! I felt the warmth of his large bony hand. The silence between us gradually deepened. The hum of the market grew louder. I felt as if all the tradesmen had come out to stand in front of their shops and look at us. All eyes were on me. And I couldn't remember the rest of the prayer. The percussive sounds coming from Salih Usta's workshop, and the soft conciliatory voice of my grandfather, calmed my fear:

'Maliki yevmiddin, iyyakenabüdü ve iyake nestain, ihtinassiratel müstakim...'[9] Those meaningless, peculiar words scurried away like black beetles, left and right, into

9. The Opening of the Qur'aan *(Al-Fatiha)* - Turkish transliteration of the Arabic.

the labyrinth of my mind. The rest immediately came back to me. Without a single stutter, I completed the Fatiha. My grandfather was so pleased! The sun shone down on the market and the tradesmen got on with their business. *Thank God I'm no longer damned! Because, if you forget even one of those words, you'll burn in hell for a year. The torments of the grave are gratis.*

I'm no longer in the market with my grandfather; I'm walking with the imam in the Bobigny Islamic cemetery. And the years are floating away, each filled with a thousand and one mysteries, just like those Arabic words. Clouds, rain clouds, disperse. Soon the sun will come out and the wet gravestones will glisten in the daylight. This is a time to speak of the living rather than the dead. But the imam is still muttering the Fatiha, while I feel like a clumsy sinner. I mustn't upset the imam. He resembles my grandfather a little, with his sparse white beard and round Adam's apple. But my grandfather was taller; I remember him as both taller and more awe-inspiring, but maybe that was because I was small. The imam glances at me as if to check whether or not I'm praying. I raise my palms to the sky and murmur something as well. Yes, something, but what? The names of dead people I knew? Or was it the lines of an ancient Persian poet? What had the Persian poet said? 'Death is impartial…'

When he finishes his prayer, the imam covers his face with the palms of his hands and says, 'Amen.' I imitate him. We start walking again. The cemetery is divided into different sections, each serving a particular category of people. For instance, right in the middle, under a pole flying the French flag, lie some Algerians who died in the war. Those who fought in the French army during their country's war of independence are called *Harki*.

'They have sixty plots,' says the imam. 'But the women and children are somewhere else.' We proceed among ancient moss-covered gravestones. Some are overturned, some half-buried in the earth, others upright and grand.

On one of them is written 'To my brother. Time passes but memories remain.' It's a nice, well-kept grave. To the right of it is a photo of a youth. A dark, handsome young man. He died when he was twenty. According to the imam, the cause of his death is uncertain. But I can guess what it was. He was either shot by the police or by a restaurant owner for not paying his bill. Or he might have been thrown out of a train window by drunken skinheads. On another gravestone is written 'We will never forget you.' A white pigeon is about to take flight from the black marble. Most of the gravestones are surrounded by stinging nettles and covered with blackthorn. We walk among discarded cans and the occasional chrysanthemum flower. 'And here,' says the imam, 'is the grave of a Turk.'

I read the inscription on the stone: 'Ahmet Fuat Cemil (1881-1955)'. The imam starts to explain:

'You Turks are also Muslims. You wouldn't want to be buried with the infidels, would you? But they've prevented us from burying anyone here for a while, on the pretext that it's full. Yet there's lots of space, as you see. It's the government – they won't allow any kind of discrimination. It's now forbidden to bury Muslims in Muslim cemeteries! So, after bathing the corpses of our religious brothers here, we have to send them back to their own countries.'

I mention to the imam that the people he refers to as 'infidels' are people who have lives similar to mine: take the same Métro, work for the same sort of boss, break the same bread.

'Fine,' he replies. 'But sharing the same soil is a different matter. Especially since it's until the Day of Judgement!' Then, perhaps wanting to change the subject, he refers to the five conditions of Islam.

'When Mohammad was alone in the cave on Mount Hira, the angel Gabriel appeared to him and called out "Iqra![10]" to which our dear Prophet said fearfully, "I know

10. Meaning 'read', and believed to be the first word of the Koran proclaimed by Gabriel to the Prophet Mohammad.

not how!" Gabriel then said "Read in the name of your Lord," and repeated it twice more. The voice of the giant-winged Gabriel caused the walls of the cave and the idols in the Kaaba to shake. Mohammad was taken by a fever and returned home, where his wife Hatice put him to bed. Then one day, again on Mount Hira, the Prophet, having not seen Gabriel for three years, was about to throw himself off a cliff, when…'

How many times have I heard this story? How many times have I heard how the Koran came down to us through divine inspiration? I heard it from my elderly grandfather in his wise judge's voice, from my grandmother who fasted not only for one month at Ramadan, but for three months, and later from my religious education teacher at school. Now, years later in Bobigny, I have no intention of listening to the same story told by a Moroccan imam in a voice that reminds me of the blind fakirs[11] in Marrakesh. I say I need to be alone for a while, so as not to hurt his feelings. He moves away without any objection, but he doesn't end our conversation with the words 'Trust in God!'

Jumping over a tree that has been upturned in a storm, I continue on my way. Trees in this country find water straight away, so they don't put down really deep roots. It doesn't take much of a storm to uproot them. On the other hand, a tree on the Anatolian plain is forced to seek out sustenance and drive roots deep into the earth in order to reach water.

To be honest, the Turk's grave shown to me by the imam was of little interest. I was seeking another one: Ali's grave. Ali, the son of Salih the blacksmith. Once again, I recall our local market: Ali and I were at the forge, looking at the furious flames. As Salih Usta worked the bellows with his long muscular arms, sparks flew up to the ceiling. Flames illuminated the blacksmith's copper-coloured face, his curly beard and sea-blue eyes, and cast a glow on pieces of iron waiting to be beaten over the fire, and on the anvil and

11. Holy men

the hammer, which lay there like a sleeping cat. When the sparks touched Salih Usta's leather apron, all the horseshoes, harnesses, knives and axes that had been tossed into a corner of the forge seemed to come to life. After beating the red-hot iron into shape, Salih used enormous tongs to plunge it into the water beside him. The iron immediately gave out a sizzling sound. In the confusion of the grey smoke that filled the shop and the bright red of the coals created by the bellows, in the dusty clouds of reds and blacks, whites and greys, I felt my heart sizzle as well.

'That's what Hell must be like,' I said to Ali.

'The fire of Hell is not like anything on Earth,' he replied. 'That fire burns a hundred times, a *thousand* times more strongly.'

Salih Usta heard what we said, despite the sound of the hammer as he brought it down with all his might onto the anvil. He smiled beneath his moustache, revealing a row of pearl-white teeth. I didn't understand why he smiled in that knowing way. Perhaps he didn't believe in Hell! Of course, he didn't. But he wouldn't say anything in front of me. He wasn't going to say to the grandson of a great judge, who never once missed Friday prayers, that Heaven and Hell exist on this Earth or that, since God will throw the rich and poor into the same fire in the other world, it is only right for us to be equally blessed in this one! The kid would only go and tell his grandfather, saying that he had heard it from the blacksmith. Salih Usta suddenly started singing. Ali and I pricked up our ears. The song kept time with the rhythm of the hammer and anvil and transported me away, beyond the ironmonger's shop and my fears of Hell's wrath, beyond the cool shade of the plane trees of the café in the market, to the plain that extends to the impoverished earth of the wasteland that is the town cemetery, to the lofty mountains and the endless Anatolian roads:

*Once more, I travel far from home.*
*Who knows where will be my tomb?*

Every time I go to Turkey, my mother never fails to caution me.

'Don't forget about the son of our late Salih,' she starts. 'That strange boy of Blacksmith Salih's. Make sure you find time this year. Go and visit his grave. He was your childhood friend.' Ali's dear mother has been sending my mother messages via anyone going to Istanbul, begging that I go and recite a Fatiha for Ali. This time, she pressed a piece of paper into my hand in an attempt to make sure that I actually went, that I had no difficulty finding it.

'Death is impartial' is written on the tombstone. I suddenly remember the second line. 'Death is impartial / It comes with the same majesty to kings and beggars alike.' At that moment, a flashbulb goes off in my memory. I recall Ali's blue eyes, like those of all his relatives. I remember his family emmigrating, their hospitality, their poverty. It's true that death is impartial, but only if life is impartial. After we moved to Istanbul, Ali left school to work as an apprentice with his father. But the ironmongery business fell into decline and his family, who had come from the Balkans to settle in that small Anatolian town, were left unemployed. After that it was France. Within three months of his arrival, when he was not yet twenty years old, a tree that he was cutting down with some other migrant workers fell on top of him. An enormous tree, bigger than the plane trees in the market café. Ali died in Orléans. His friends couldn't raise enough money between them to send his body back to Turkey, so he was buried here at the Islamic Cemetery in Bobigny. It was 1971. That means that Ali, my school friend Ali, had come to France in the same year as I did. He started working at a timber yard in Orléans while I was registering at the Sorbonne. What was it the ancient Persian said? 'Death is impartial / It comes with the same majesty to kings and

35

beggars alike.'

Death came to Ali with the majesty of a falling tree. Death, where is your justice? Where is Brother Nazim, whose words keep haunting me from his grave in Moscow? Where is my grandfather's brother who never returned from Yemen? Where are the uncles in Skopje and my grandmother's grandfather who lies with Ali's ancestors in Shumen. Where are they all? Those who depart and never return, those who mean to return but don't make it, the stateless, the Greek mystics who carried nothing in their food bags but the Turkish language. Where are you, my friends? You have long turned to dust in the four corners of the Earth! I couldn't find Ali's grave. If I'd found it, I would have erased the lines of the Persian poet and written on his gravestone the words sung by Blacksmith Salih:

*Once more, I travel far from home.*
*Who knows where will be my tomb?*

# The Airport

The world has grown smaller; travel is something I've become accustomed to. I'm at Roissy Airport. Aeroplanes take off to all parts of the world. New York, Tokyo, Moscow, Istanbul. A woman's metallic voice. The same voice, the same language everywhere, in every country. Yet the women I've loved laugh and cry in different languages. A hotel room where we slept, curled up together, without getting between the sheets. An empty bed in the moonlight, clothes on hangers. When the window is opened, the room fills with stars and I cover my nakedness with their celestial bodies, full of desire and insatiable. Tram stops where we say farewell, narrow streets leading down to the sea and long, long roads. And my unwritten letters, the 'don't forget me' telegrams, the storms.

Yes, this morning I heard on the radio that the roads there are covered in snow. Even if I wanted to, I could not go to her. My window – our window – looked out on a magnificent tree that had taken root in the garden. When the first bird of the new year alighted on one of its branches, I – we – had not woken up alone. The tresses of her hair that fell over my face were framed in two mirrors on two walls simultaneously. Did the first – almost feline – steps of separation enter with the daylight through the window? Separation: a fear that approached with stealthy, furtive steps. I could have stayed in the comfort of the warm house that reminded me of Calypso's cave. I could have passed the rest of my days far away from Paris, in the shade of that magnificent tree in the garden. I could have combined my days with your days. But, as I set out for my morning walk, a voice, always the same voice, whispered in my ear, 'You are destined to go back!'

So, I'm on my way back, completely alone, on the threshold of an exit. Back there, I would be awaited by bowls of lovely soup, and a woman at the window. But where that place is, I don't really know. What I know about is absence; the endless geography of yearning. What I know about is trains passing through stations without stopping and the waiting rooms left behind. This time, I shall go through the door. The door I have taken you through countless times. Through the narrow door. And the abyss that swallowed us up will open before me. Do you know what the flower said when it opened in an abyss?[12] 'Abyss, you are where I belong!'[13] So said a poet in his light delicate voice, a poet who died a premature death.

Concorde passengers are passing through the glass partition, en route to New York. I have a deep uneasiness, the like of which I never feel anywhere else, in the airless vacuum of those concertina-like neon-lit gangways. However, I am sitting here with you at the airport, with a cup of coffee. Silent, with you. Soon I shall walk down that gangway and head for another city - maybe Istanbul, maybe not. What a shame that Istanbul has become a city I go to rather than return to. The same applies to Paris. I'm always going to places, never returning. As always, there are smartly dressed women, air hostesses and handsome pilots around. And of course the Japanese. I read that a Japanese businessman threw himself off the Bosphorus Bridge. He just never made it to the other side. How many times have I crossed that bridge? The bridge, which I've seen sparkling at night and that gives Istanbul its best silhouette during the day. Have I been living

12. Penultimate line of *Yurdumsun ey uçurum!* [Abyss, you are where I belong] by Cemal Süreya 1931-1990.
13. Title and last line of the above poem.

as if on a bridge? Between two continents, two languages, two women? Perhaps I am a bridge, a causeway, without solid foundations. Neither there nor here. Both there and here. But bridges help to keep everything going. Rivers flow beneath them, torrents of traffic on them. The bridges of New York, Paris and Istanbul. On the plain, there's a bridge designed by Sinan over a dried up river; and another one that binds young sweethearts by linking one shore to another. I've always loved bridges, even if they don't lead me to you. Except for the one on the River Charles, because the river was always freezing over and your hand kept slipping out of mine when we crossed its steel-girdered structure.

Great, the planes are taking off! Planes are taking off right next to the coffee cups. It's so easy, they're so light. They go up and down like gulls in the blue over the Bosphorus. It's nine o'clock, nine o'clock exactly. The metallic voice has announced the departure of a flight to Glasgow, followed by a flight to Amsterdam. I've never been to Glasgow. It's almost certainly raining; in the wet streets, traffic lights change from red to amber and then to green. Exhausted black cars crawl patiently like ants in the busy traffic. It's true; I've never been to Glasgow, or to any of Britain's dilapidated cities, apart from London. But of course, I've been to Oxford and Cambridge. How quickly I'd forgotten. Clearly some cities leave very little trace. Like some people, some books and most lovemaking. But I remember London. The gush of light in Turner's paintings at the National Gallery. The masterpieces of Uccello and Botticelli, and the long, thin face of our white-turbaned Fatih. I don't remember seeing another face in the mirror at the hotel overlooking Hyde Park. I must have forgotten that face. I must have forgotten the happiness of waking up together and walking through the streets of London in the rain. I've never been to Glasgow, but I know the canals of Amsterdam like the back of my hand. Women displayed in shop windows, trees shedding autumn leaves. The harmony of water, bricks and glass. Were the leaves shed by the trees in Amsterdam or by the shivering bodies as they stripped? Maybe neither. Maybe it was just the clear grey light that made us light-hearted, like leaves flying in the air. We walked and walked in Vermeer's light before interlocking and shedding our leaves.

I suddenly recalled going from Roissy Airport to New York; it was not long ago, a mere two years. I woke up the next day in the Roosevelt Hotel on Madison Avenue. I spent the whole day wandering around the city. I've written numerous times about my impressions of New York, but never about our encounter. When I returned to the hotel in the evening, I stretched out on the bed with a whisky on the rocks. Your voice sounded anxious on the telephone.

'I see you've started drinking early!'

'How could you tell?'

'I can hear the ice clinking.'

I moved the glass in my hand away from the telephone receiver. First we spoke about this and that. The house needed repainting; one of the cats had run away. The days were going quite well. Yes, you'd missed me a lot, but you couldn't come immediately. Maybe you'd be on the first flight tomorrow, maybe next time. Now, you're no longer even a voice on the telephone.

I suddenly recalled going from Roissy Airport to Istanbul. I woke up the next day in Anadoluhisari. I've written numerous times about this, about my returns that were not really returns, about the Bosphorus Bridge that I never quite managed to reach, about the chiming clock that competed with time in the bedroom of my childhood. How often that clock failed to chime! When I awoke, the daylight that came through the drawn curtains wasn't reflected on the ceiling as usual. The room was in darkness. I didn't hear the sound of ferries starting up at dawn. Darkness spread from the floor to the bed and on towards the table. I saw the wall. It was not where it had been before. Nor was the table. The papers that had been on it were disappearing. I remained motionless in the bed. It was light outside. But somehow the light shining on the window did not penetrate the room. Things seemed to be moving away from each other in the darkness, the source of which I couldn't fathom. The table, the chair, the chiming clock on the bookshelf. I noticed that it had no hour hand. I thought about the loneliness of the minute hand. They were things that complemented one another, that were useless and totally non-functional if separated from each other. Needle and thread, bullet and gun, hammer and nail. And I thought of people, famous lovers. Leyla and Mecnun, Romeo and Juliet, Kerem and Asli, Ferhat and Sirin. Woman and man. But the loneliness of the hour hand was something quite different, a frightening separation. I felt a sudden urge to draw the curtains and see what the time was. Then I couldn't be bothered. I fell asleep.

The world has grown smaller; travel is something I've grown accustomed to. I'm at Roissy Airport. Before this airport was built, I used to go to Istanbul from Orly. For years after the September 12th coup, I couldn't go back to Turkey so I travelled to Tunisia, Greece and Algeria. On another trip, I saw a plane belonging to Argentine Airways that was about to take off. Its name was 'Diyarbakir',[14] its destination: Istanbul.

14. City in south east Turkey.

# Death in a Wheatfield

DEATH HAD PREVIOUSLY confronted him as a bullet from the threshing floor. And now, years later, here he is in a museum, peering at a painting of ears of wheat blowing in the wind.[15] In the July sunshine the grain, swept up as if by a storm, will soon be reduced to pickings for the crows. But the wheat field with the track running through it is merely paint, and so are the crows that swoop over the grain. They fly off as if to escape not a bullet, but the painter's own loneliness, his increasingly irritable obsession with work, the flames of hell. To escape before the painter can use his brush to spread them across the canvas. His fingers, strong from not having touched a woman in months, have poured all his pain, his desire for death and his self-destructiveness into this picture. He has mixed and composed his colours as if kneading clay for a statue. He has created crows from his hallucinations, an indigo sky from his sleepless nights, puffy white clouds and ears of wheat from his hopeless insanity. Then set all these colours against each other and deserted this incompatible world.

Death takes one look at everyone. But it is looking at this man for a second time.

A gun had been fired on that afternoon.

'The house is surrounded. Give yourself up!'

Yet here, there is no sign of a gendarme, no finger on a trigger. The danger might have been from the crows, but they are only painted. A wheat field, a deserted track and a

15. 'Wheat Field with Crows', 1890, one of Van Gogh's last paintings, in the Van Gogh Museum, Amsterdam.

sky. That's all. And the natural, liberating light of imminent death in a landscape without people.

Outside the picture, the painter holds the gun to his heart. It will soon be fired. Perhaps more black crows will fly up through the ears of wheat; perhaps they will blacken the sky.

For the man, too, death had arrived in the shape of a bullet, but it ricocheted from a crack in the glass and whizzed past his head.

'The house is surrounded. Give yourself up!'

If he had stirred, the second bullet would have got him in the middle of his forehead. If he had thought his voice could be heard from hundreds of kilometres away, he would have shouted out to Sehmuz that this was too high a price to pay for being a writer. Sehmuz's father had walked towards the window and calmly said, 'Don't be afraid. I'll distract them. There won't be more than two of them. They can't have surrounded the house. We'll all escape together when it gets dark.' He used the Kalashnikov - which he cleaned and wiped every day with the tenderness of a mother changing a baby's nappy - to fire back at the gendarmes who had been shooting from the threshing floor. As soon as darkness fell, he led the way out. They climbed over the wall of the back courtyard, walked to another village and on to the border. It was not customary for these people to deliver up anyone sheltering under their roof. Naturally, when Sehmuz had sent him the news from prison, he had had no way of knowing that he would hide for weeks in the guest room of a mud-clad house in the southeast, living with smugglers about whom he had known nothing until then, except for novels, laments and folk-songs that told of adventures ending in death.

Sehmuz was the eldest son of an impoverished family. Somehow or other, he had been able get away; instead of becoming a smuggler like his brothers, he had managed to complete his education and settle in Istanbul, where he now had a family. But he could not find peace of mind. He joined left-wing demonstrations and was arrested and imprisoned a few times; he lost his job and, in order to keep his family, became a street vendor. The two of them had first met when Sehmuz was selling cut-price books on Cagaloglu Yokus, including some of his own earlier books. Those were the days when not only books but socialism too was sold cheaply, when political crime escalated. They were fertile days, when he loved to prowl like a wolf for material he could later use in a story. They had soon become friends and decided to write a novel together, an adventure story that would break all sales records. They would set out the harsh realities of the southeast in an abrasive manner, using a technique that was half documentary, half fiction, in an attempt to penetrate the tragedies of daily life in the region. Naturally, they would use the world of smugglers as the basis of this tragedy. They would tell how landless peasants were pushed into smuggling in order to make ends meet; how the millions that were earned were shared between intermediaries and corrupt government officials; how there were people who had diced with death in the minefields, like pawns on a chessboard, who now limped around the village squares; about the rising number of gangs of one-armed men, not only in that area, but in the country as a whole. Sehmuz would tell the story of his childhood: of the magic of the goods he smuggled over the border; of the night-time sounds of bullets and mules' hooves; of how his younger brother tripped on a mine and lost a leg; of bravery and cowardice, love and death, friendship and treachery.

He cannot take his eyes off the wheat field. He is face-to-face with death. Yet before, when that bullet whizzed above his head and struck the wall, he had not felt so close to death. When he was crossing the border that night, it had never even occurred to him that he might step on a mine and be blown to bits. However, for some reason, in the museum that bears the name of this crazy artist and exhibits his creative genius, death is now peering right at him through the ears of wheat. It draws him inward towards his own reality. How startling silence is. A gunshot seems to flare within himself rather than in the picture. He remembers seeing nobody on the threshing floor. Harvested crops, a village, low-slung houses and dusty streets which, in the smoke of dried dung burning on the roofs, were forged into a reality that he did not recognise, nor did he make any attempt to do so. Only Sehmuz could have written about that reality. If, one day, he got out of prison, if the hand that had been broken under torture could hold a pen, he would be able to write in the language of the locals about the semi-naked children playing in the courtyard, the women by the hearth, the sorrow on the men's furrowed, sun-burned faces, the endless arid plain that reverberated with the sounds of Mausers and Kalashnikovs, the dogs that howled at night, the houses, the larders, and the scorpions and centipedes that occupied secret corners of the wooden balconies. Like a lamentation, it would be aflame with inner grief. This was a world where he had never felt at home, a world he did not understand. When walking in a wheat field, not once had he ever looked up at the sky through grains of wheat. And if he had done, he would have felt no excitement. Only form and colour excited him, not reality itself.

Yes, he thought, one day, Sehmuz will write about the southeast. About the rust-coloured houses, the dark walls, the flocks of sheep and the gas lamps – a world of people living in another century. Mountain villages accessible only by mule. The fear and treachery.

He remembered the guest room in the village house where he had hidden for weeks on end. On the wall had been an old photograph of Sehmuz and his siblings. Two dilapidated armchairs, embroidered cushions on the divan. An old kilim on the floor. When the first bullet broke the window and bounced off the opposite wall, he had thrown himself to the floor as instructed by Sehmuz's father; he did not move a muscle until darkness fell. That was why he remembered the smell and colours of the kilim so well. It was a strange smell. It had the texture of dried leaves, and a fragrance that gradually enveloped and anaesthetized him. Or did the kilim have the smell of death? But at that time, he had not thought about death; it had never even crossed his mind.

Later, when he was in the minefield, he had thought about the death of others, but not his own. In the darkness of night, death was an abstract concept, but here in the wheat field, expressed from the artist's tubes of paint, it turned into reality, into an irrecoverable sorrow that he felt in the depths of his being.

He writhes in sorrow now, as if he wants to extract from his own heart the bullet that entered the heart of the painter on one summer afternoon. The weapon fired from the threshing floor was no more real than the echo of the invisible gun in the picture; this he understands better as time passes. Each day gets a little better. True, he does not know how to spend his days. In the crowded streets of foreign towns, in the loneliness of nights spent in hotel bedrooms and daytimes in waterside cafés, far away from his country, from the woman he loves and his mother tongue - the days seem endless. But he tiptoes through these days like a ballerina, without leaving any footprints. Turkish words, his own words, are tossed by the wind, dying before they can scatter their seed.

# By the Lake

THEY WERE SITTING at a café by the lake; the café was shaded by pergolas, and the legs of their table were almost in the indigo-blue water. The sun had not yet begun to pale towards the bare peaks around the lake. It seemed about to burst in the cloudless sky. They were alone in the shade of the pergola. It was rare for anyone to come to this lakeside café before sunset, even though it was only a few kilometres outside the city. They had disturbed the waiter from his midday nap and ordered two medium-sweet Turkish coffees. An enormous horsefly flew around their empty coffee cups, its penetrating buzz piercing their brains. The woman flicked angrily at it with her hand. The fly took off from the table, did a tour of the man's shaved head, headed for the woman and landed right on the end of her nose.

*She hasn't changed at all,* thought the man. *She's as pert, arrogant, perverse and lovely as ever...* He wanted to caress the woman's long black hair and say, 'This is good. I'm so happy.' However, seeing an argumentative look appear in her pensive eyes, he refrained from saying anything. Instead, he lit a cigarette and inhaled the smoke deep into his lungs. The fly flew away from the woman's nose.

'That's the third one,' she said. 'You've become a heavy smoker since we last saw each other.'

The man did not answer. For a while, he just listened to the flow of comments coming from the woman's mouth. She was speaking in a language that he understood but had not spoken for months; that he had not forgotten but had thought he would never hear again. It was soft and beautiful, a nasal language. Long ago, maybe years ago, her voice had whispered words of passion in his ear in the dark.

'It's not really that long since we saw each other,' continued the woman, 'but it seems long to me…'

The man had been living in a magnificent, sparkling European city, but now spent his time shut up in these remote barracks and had lost all sense of time. He thought about the midday muster. They were gathered on the parade ground, standing to attention. The commander had not yet appeared. The sun was burning the tops of their heads even more ferociously than usual. He recalled the large red ears of the man standing in front of him. His cap was unable to cover those strange ears hanging on both sides of his lumpy shaved head. They were covered in cuts and bruises, like docile animals dying in the heat.

The man's ability to fall asleep the moment his head touched the pillow at night had left him long ago. His own ears were covered in festering sores from the sun and he could no longer sleep on them. In the cool of the night, he killed time by looking through the open window at the stars above the plain. In the early hours, daylight would shine on his grim, lined face. After a tired, sleepless night, instead of welcoming the start of a new day, he would use his bayonet to scratch yet another mark on the metal frame of his bunk bed. Each mark indicated the beginning of a day, not the end. The days did not end as they had started. And each muster was different. The morning muster took place in a milky white light that shone on the mountains opposite, the midday muster under a sun that roasted their brains, and the evening muster seemed to go on forever, in the lengthening shadows of the barrels of their rifles, their bodies struggling to remain upright. 'At ease - Attention - Shoulder Arms - Present arms - Stand at ease - Attention - Present Arms - Shoulder arms - At ease!'

His repertoire of words was gradually shrinking, leaving little else in his memory apart from an odd collection of commands. 'Rise and shine! Quick march – Left right, left right, left right! Halt!' This was partly why he did not speak.

Where should he start? How should he talk about that remote world to this woman who knew nothing about it, and never would? How should he explain the nightmare, which she was only ever likely to experience in a midday sleep? In which language, with which words, which screams?

'Do you want another coffee?' he asked.

He thought the woman must be tolerating this mud-coloured coffee, which bore no resemblance to the coffee in her own country, because of her affection for him. But what about the other things? What about the lack of running water, the heat, the dirty toilets, the sound of the call to prayer, the crowds of men? Would she put up with these because she could not give him up?

'Yes,' she said in a voice that was as soft as silk.

The man called the waiter. As he ordered two more medium-sweet coffees, he noticed an unexpected change in the tone of his voice: it had acquired a tyrannical, severe quality.

'Did you hear that?' he asked the woman. 'Did you hear the way I spoke to him?'

'I heard you. What of it?'

'Didn't you notice anything different?'

'What was I supposed to notice?'

'My tone of voice. I ordered the coffees as if I was giving him orders.'

'I didn't notice. Maybe it's because I don't know Turkish.'

The man understood for the first time that it was not the thousands of miles of road or the barrier of wire-fencing that separated them, but their words.

'If only you'd learned Turkish, you wouldn't have been so remote and indifferent,' he complained. 'You'd have understood me better.'

The woman suddenly looked annoyed. She fixed her eyes on the man's chubby face and said, 'Look darling, I came all this way to see you, even though it's only for an hour or so, but I didn't come to listen to your stupid complaints!'

The man imagined the woman boarding the plane at the airport. Next to her was the lover she was keeping secret from him. They would have spent the night together and woken up side by side. Yes, that must be what had happened. It was obvious from her sparkling eyes and relaxed posture. Then he thought of her in Istanbul, where she is waiting for a bus at Harem. The white clothes she is wearing are not yet dirty. She is sitting in the bus station café overlooking the sea. The city is bathed in light. The Maiden's Tower, the ships entering the Bosphorus, and the minarets on the opposite shore are a gleaming white. Like her white undulating body when making passionate love and gleaming with perspiration in the dark. She is alone on a smoke-filled night-bus. She sits down next to a window and looks out. In the light from the window, the road looks desolate. Occasionally, a timber-laden truck rumbles past, dangerously close. Then, tractors loaded with labourers going out to the tobacco fields. As dawn breaks, the bus starts across the plain. Now, flat earth and the occasional poplar tree stream past the window while, in the distance, bare peaks are already starting to burn in the morning sun.

'Forgive me,' said the man. 'I didn't know you'd come so far for my sake. I wasn't being fair on you.'

The woman raised her hand, which had been resting next to the empty coffee cup, and let it wander over the man's burnt face and chapped, split lips. Then, lovingly, without a hint of hesitation, she stroked his shaved head. Yet, a short while before, when waiting in front of the main gate, she had not recognised him among the crowd of soldiers coming out of the barracks. They all looked identical in their combat boots and caps. And with loneliness in their tired, dull eyes. They had descended on the lively, singing bars of the city like a swarm of locusts. He was among the last to come out.

'The dancer shouted out "Hey, handsome skinheads!" to you!' she said.

Her hand was still resting on the man's head. He had joked about her difficulty in recognising him and had then told her how, after the dancer shouted out, 'Hey, handsome skinheads,' he had removed first her bra and then her panties, on entertainment night at the barracks. But now, he was out on leave and he did not want to remember that night, especially in front of another woman.

'Yep, she did,' he said abruptly. With his calloused fingers, he grasped the hand that was stroking his head, brought it to his lips and kissed it. Then he put it back in the same place on the table. For a while he wallowed in a soft feeling which spread from his lips to his tongue and from there right through his body. He felt the woman's pale hand deep, deep inside him. At the same moment, he felt a stirring in his groin. He clasped the hand on the table again and, drawing it towards him beneath the tablecloth, pressed it over his hardening penis. They remained like that for a moment. The woman smiled; a gleam appeared in her eyes and then faded.

'I missed you so much,' she whispered to the man.

The man remembered the sign that greeted them as they wandered past the hotels - three of them in total - on the main road. The black letters of those awful words were imprinted on his memory: PRIVATES AND CONSCRIPTS FORBIDDEN. His penis softened and shrank; the woman, who had been smiling wickedly at him, gradually moved away. She withdrew her hand from his and seemed to him to be stroking another man in another city. Yet her hand was still under the table.

'I missed you so much,' she repeated. 'Your smell, your skin, your hardness inside me.'

Her voice was full of desire. So were her eyes - warm

and loving. As if she were talking to someone else. As if they were not sitting under a pergola in a café by the lake. As if, when the waiter brought their coffees, they would not be sitting there hand in hand like that, caressing each other under the table.

'I missed you a lot too, at first,' said the man. 'Then I forgot. I forgot everything. I forgot there was another world outside the barracks.'

The woman did not hear. She was still trying to revive the man's wilting penis.

'It's different with you,' she was saying to him. 'I want you so much. I want you more than ever!'

She was trying to undo the buttons on his trousers, which were thick with dirt.

'I'll wait for you,' she said. 'I'll wait for you until you return and you're mine again. Hold me! Come, hold me and enter me! Right now. Enter me, now!'

'Shut up, stop talking,' hissed the man in a harsh voice.

He pulled the woman's hand away and pushed his chair back. At that moment, the woman felt as abandoned as the arid peaks around the lake. She wanted to immerse her burning, naked body in the cool waters of the lake, to dissolve completely in its indigo blueness. Then the man spoke gently, in a defeated tone. 'Let's go,' he said. 'There isn't much time.'

They left the café and walked along the dusty road to the barracks. The sun beat down on their heads.

# The Tunnel

*THE MODANE-FRÉJUS Tunnel is twelve thousand five hundred metres long — but not for everyone.*

No, that's terrible. I must find a different sentence.

*Trains come and go and I remain here involved in my own problems.*

No good at all! It's badly constructed and too emotional. The sentence should be spare and striking. I'm sitting by the window on the Strasbourg-Paris train, thinking. I must find an arresting sentence with no frills: a perfect sentence. Trees fly past by the window. Carefully tilled fields, well-fed cows and canals pass by. I'm not interested in any of them. The train races along its tracks. We leave behind deserted stations and the boredom of waiting rooms. Then, more trees, fields and yet more fields... For a while, we see a large expanse of sky. I notice the bell tower of a church in the distance. The iron cockerel atop its belfry challenges the clouds. We go past villages. Pretty, well-kept villages, whose cockerels are now merely part of their history. Walls, windows, houses with gardens. Soon, house lights will come on, doors will be closed and curtains drawn. There will be nobody about. I think about deserted streets and empty cafés. Night will suddenly descend over the roofs; darkness will envelop the gardens and houses. Inside, in their lighted sitting rooms, people will forget about the hostile night and their loneliness.

*From a mud-roofed village house on one side of the tunnel, to a five-roomed apartment on the other.*

Not bad. It has a suggestion of yearning, of a dream, of

darkness reaching out to light.

'What is it, old man?' asks Jacques. 'You've gone very quiet.'

He startles me. I'd forgotten that Jacques is sitting next to me. He always calls me 'old man'. Yet we're the same age. He's called me 'old man' ever since we became friends, perhaps to emphasise our closeness.

'I'm thinking about the first sentence, Jacques. The first sentence is very important.'

'No! Wherever did you get that idea from? What's it the first sentence of?'

'What do you think? Our soundtrack.'

'Never mind the soundtrack. Just listen to me.'

He sips his coffee. How comfortable he looks, with that pipe which never leaves his mouth. Everything about him marks him out as a professional journalist and successful television producer.

'I'll order you a coffee,' he says, 'otherwise you're going to nod off.'

'Look Jacques, we could start like this: "Every tunnel welcomes the daylight; it punctuates the darkness with hope. From a mud-roofed village house on one side of the tunnel, to a five-roomed apartment on the other."'

Jacques draws deeply on his pipe. 'Look, my dear writer,' he says. 'This is different. It's not like writing a novel. It all comes together in the editing. You'll never find the first sentence before you've settled on the first image. Or if you do, it'll be no good.'

Jacques is right: cinema is different. I realise that, as a writer, I attach too much importance to the first sentence. I need to break this habit immediately. The narrative must be through images, not words. I must get used to thinking and writing in images. A dark, forbidding tunnel entrance. That must be the first image. Then, a train lit up inside. In the following scene, we'll see carriages with passengers sitting comfortably in their seats, reading newspapers or looking out of the window. In the sea of colour that goes by, there'll be pretty women, with pampered, made-up faces. Everyone looking happy and confident. The passengers must appear excited about going to some unknown, unattainable world, about travelling from one city to another, one country to another. Rather than the monotony of daily life, the journey should conjure up excitement, mixed with a tinge of melancholy at leaving behind people and things that are dear. The camera will zoom in as the train goes into the darkness of the tunnel. In the next shot, we'll see the train all lit up again. Then it will suddenly disappear into the darkness. The happy lit-up world is extinguished, and the magic of the journey evaporates. Lightning strikes, like a sharp sickle of death cutting through a promising dream.

'You're right, Jacques,' I say to my friend. 'Above all else, cinema means images. The main issue isn't words, but forming a chain of images through editing.'

Jacques smiles beneath his moustache and says, 'We know you're a professor at the Sorbonne, old man! But teaching is one thing and making films is another. You don't really understand this business.'

'Look, just listen to me. Listen to what I have to say, and then tell me to sod off if you want.'

I explain the outline of the first three shots to Jacques. 'I knew you wouldn't be able to manage this,' he says, smiling in his usual mocking way. 'You've already forgotten how limited our resources are!'

It's true. We hadn't been able to film the passengers in the carriages. While we were waiting for a train to pass, it had grown dark at the tunnel entrance. We had previously shot a view of the tunnel from the front of a train, and our sound technicians had recorded the rumble of wheels on the railway lines. But to shoot inside the carriages, the camera needed to be positioned high up and, while we waited for a second train to pass, the wintry sun had suddenly gone down and it was dark. I had no idea of course that darkness would descend so quickly in Alsace, and that it would leave us unable to do anything. When the lighting engineer said we needed to come back early the following day, Jacques said, 'Time's too short. We'll have to abandon this scene.'

Yet I've prepared a text for this scene and, in my imagination, I've added more images of the train journey. Jacques had told me that the tunnel is at least sixty kilometres from Strasbourg, so all the tunnel and train scenes would have to be shot in one day. And what he says goes; he's not a director to be argued with.

He's now distancing himself in that way he knows only too well. He wants to squeeze me out of the work we're supposed to be doing together. He'll make his film and do the editing first; then, when the film is ready, he'll ask me to write a bit of text for a few of the scenes.

'Look, Jacques,' I say. 'You're an egotist and a smartass, like all directors. But I'm not going to give in over this so easily. We'll do the editing together.'

'And you,' he says, raising his voice, 'you're stubborn and a mythomaniac. You go off on a tangent like all writers!' Then he softens his voice: 'Of course you can come to the studio, if you want. But you'd do well to leave the job of editing to the director.'

I decide there's no need to explain to Jacques that a writer's job also involves editing and that, despite the different medium, there's not so much difference between linking images and putting what you want to convey into written language. Jacques empties his pipe, refills it and leans back in his seat. He nods off immediately. He may not manage to make up for the tiredness of a week's filming by the time we get to Paris, but he can at least doze a little and collect his thoughts. Does he care about the real world? Osman, Emine, Aynur, Faruk, Aysel... For him, they're all just ingredients. And me? What about me? After a week of intensive work, I'm at loggerheads with him again.

MUSTAFA:
Osman and I were going to create a garden here together,
but it wasn't to be.

ANDRÉ THORAVAL
[Bisheim Community Residential Management official]:
We finally gave Mr Coci a five-bedroomed apartment, but
I didn't see him again.

IBRAHIM THE GROCER
[His voice is thick with the aroma of pastrami and opium]:
Osman used to come into the shop occasionally and have a
chat with me.

IMAM HÜSEYIN:
Fate! It was my brother's fate. God bless the poor bereaved.

RENÉ KOHLER
[Unemployment Benefits Manager]:
I have Mr Osman Coci's card here, but I never actually
met him.

CLAUDE HERMIER
[Strasbourg Province Foreign Workers official]:
The law is incontrovertibly clear. We learnt about the
incident from the newspapers.

FRANÇOISE DUPEYRAT
[Foreign Workers' Solidarity Committee Secretary]:
The regulations are responsible for this incident. It's the
French formalities that killed the Coci family.

THE TURKISH CONSUL IN STRASBOURG:
Osman was a victim of the visa system. The French
government should lift the visa requirement for Turks.

Aynur
[Looking up with large, moss green eyes]:
The train went crazy. It took my Daddy away.

Faruk:
The trains took my mother and my brother and sisters
away. I hate trains.

[Aysel says nothing. Even a knife wouldn't prise open
her mouth. She trembles constantly on her bed at the
clinic. Osman Coci is of course silent. Emine, Ömer and
Gülnur say nothing either.]

Mustafa:
Osman was closer to me than a brother. I broke down in
tears when I was washing his corpse. All that was left of
our Osman, that big strapping young man, was a pile of
dismembered meat.

Strasbourg Safety official:
The children are now with their uncle. We're unable to
give them residency permits.

Policewoman [Coquettishly]:
That's right, we can't. It would be against the law.
[She goes back to her typing.]

Turkish Consul:
Their uncle, Imam Hüseyin, is prepared to have the
children if the French authorities will permit it.

Official
[In a metallic sounding voice]:
These children must be sent back to Turkey. Under
French law, from a legal perspective, we cannot accept the
presence of these children.

They end up making 'non-persons' of the children. Yet I saw them with my own eyes – they were real. Aysel's face was bright yellow on the bed. Aynur was playing tag in the street. Faruk asked us for a bicycle. We promised to bring him a bicycle on our next visit. But we won't go to Strasbourg again. Our work is over, really. We've finished the shooting and turned the children into props. Not just the children! Into those few square centimetres of frame, we've also managed to fit Osman Coci's friend Mustafa, a few images of the housing estate in Bisheim, the children's uncle, Imam Hüseyin, the canals, the narrow streets and even the rust-coloured walls of the cathedral in Strasbourg where Coci spent years of his life. But there is so much more that we've excluded. Aysel's frightened olive-black eyes, the faded writing on the worn pages of a Koran, the drawn, humble face of Imam Hüseyin reading the 'Fatiha' in a mosque…

We've gathered together some photos of the plain from archives. Mud-clad houses, children leaping about in a threshing field, the sorrowful face of a woman drawing water from a well. Then, the loneliness of mountains and fields. Labour markets, trucks, horse-drawn carts and sick, exhausted donkeys. We've also found some photographs of poplars swaying in the wind as a background for these people from the Anatolian plains. Decorated poplars, tractors adorned like brides, dry cracked earth, a single tree on the plain – we have everything we need to convey Osman's world, even the latest songs of exile. It'll be easy now. Jacques will sort out the editing and bring it all together. He'll do his best to relay to the French audience the incredible adventure of a Turkish worker's family and the tragic end of Osman Coci, Emine Coci and their children Ömer, Gülnur and Aysel, with the least possible emotion or melodrama. For Jacques, it is important to convey how the Coci family managed to come all the way from a central Anatolian village and reach the Fréjus Tunnel on the Italian-French border. After explaining the social and economic forces behind this, he'll make it clear that the French authorities were partly to blame. And if they are found to have any such responsibility, he will criticise France, the cradle of human rights, without delving too deeply into the matter, because the foreign workers issue can only be discussed up to a certain point on television.

But I'm thinking about you, Osman. I'm thinking about the mansions and large airy houses you worked on as a bricklayer for ten years, but never lived in. A river flows between the mountains. As Orhan Veli says, 'Death is God's will / But if only there were no separation.' A river flows by, through years of separations. I think of his loneliness in a cold attic room in Strasbourg. Houses and rooms on whose whitewashed walls hang small treasures brought there by your Anatolian hands, Osman. It's not a docile river like those in France, but a wild, turbid river, foaming at the bottom of its steep banks. A river with a current strong enough to take you from your village, from your homeland, to your lonely life in a Strasbourg attic room, to the blues, reds and greens of the merry-go-round life of a foreigner. A crazy river which uproots your wife and children and carries them away from the countryside, leaving them like unwanted dregs in an Istanbul shanty town, in rooms with broken windows and peeling plaster. I must make a reference to this river.

'Jacques,' I say. 'What if we start with the image of a river? Then there could be a voiceover saying, "Death is God's will / But if only there were no separation," and a few lines of an Anatolian folk song. What do you think?'

'Too emotional, old man! We don't want to make the French cry; we want to find out who's responsible and expose them. We haven't collected all this material for nothing!'

Does Jacques care about Osman? What is the loneliness, the desolation of a foreign worker to him? Jacques is first and foremost a journalist, a hunter on the prowl. As for me, I'm on the Strasbourg-Paris train thinking about you, Osman. The world flows by outside. Houses, streets and bridges. It will soon be dark and evening will have come. An evening in France that bears no similarity to the evenings in your village. I think of the evenings you have spent in exile. Cold Strasbourg evenings. The dim lamp you switched on when the snow beat against the window. Tea brewing on the stove, a picture of the Bosphorus Bridge on the wall. And in the corner, a photo of your children by your bed. In front, the girls holding hands; behind, the boys and their mother. They are looking into the distance, into the loneliness of your room. I'm thinking of you, Osman. The fires you lit on the plain years ago, the village youths you wrestled with and the stars that suddenly filled the world as the shadows lengthened. Then, the light of your torch in the tunnel. The light penetrates the darkness, lighting up the damp, soot-covered walls. As you walk, the light goes before you. You shine the torch on the bolts of the rails. Every so often, you call out to Emine who is following behind, holding onto the children's hands. Mustafa said that you told them 'We're nearly there, my darlings' in order to give them courage. Whenever a train went past, they had pressed themselves against the tunnel wall; that was why your palms were all sooty. Mustafa said he was unable to wash away all the soot from your corpses.

When we reached Paris, my ears were humming. As we waited for a taxi at the station, Jacques pulled a sheaf of papers out of his inside jacket pocket and handed it to me.

'All that effort for nothing, old man! But why not write a drama about the Coci family? I've no idea whether it should be a lament, a short story or a novel. But this is the text we'll use for the film.'

He gives me the following text in French to read and edit:

Osman Coci was from a rural village in Turkey. He moved with his family to Istanbul; unable to find work there, he came to France. For ten years, he worked as a bricklayer on construction sites in Strasbourg. His application for his wife Emine Coci and their children, Aysel, Gülnur, Aynur, Faruk and Ömer, to join him was accepted, and the Strasbourg Municipality allocated him a five-roomed, self-contained flat, on the condition that he lived there with his family. However, after all those years of waiting, Mr Coci was suddenly made redundant. This meant that, despite having a place to live, he had lost the legal right to have his family with him. When the French government refused to grant visas for the Coci family, Osman decided to smuggle his wife and children into our country across the Italian border. The youngest children, Aynur and Faruk, crossed the border hidden in the boot of a car owned by Mustafa, Osman's childhood friend from the same village, who had also worked as a bricklayer for ten years in Strasbourg. The remaining members of the family, that is the mother, father and three children, entered the Modane-Fréjus Tunnel, carrying essential provisions. The tunnel is twelve thousand five hundred metres long. It is a rail link between Italy and France, and is a busy border crossing point. Mustafa and the youngest children, Aynur and Faruk, waited for Osman Coci and his family to emerge from the tunnel. According to Mustafa, they waited a long time and then a light appeared in the darkness of the tunnel. Aynur and Faruk were very happy to see this. It meant they would soon be reunited with their siblings. But just then, a train heading for Italy smashed the Coci family to smithereens five hundred metres from the tunnel exit. Only Aysel survived the accident. What follows is an investigative documentary from our Strasburg team that will bring to light facts that have hitherto been shrouded in darkness.

# The Well of Chains; a Graveyard of Unwritten Books

UNTIL MY MOVE to rue du Figuier in Paris, I'd viewed writing as a way of life. I still feel the same way yet, despite my need as a writer to integrate with the world and its people, to feel the pulse of nature and society, including the sea, the streets, the cities, the children and trees, the earth and birds, night and day, my move to this street of ancient buildings has imposed on me a certain loneliness that is gradually becoming obsessive. I'm no longer as tolerant and free in my relationship with words. I don't easily give in to the movement of words that pirouette and alight on the top of my head like little moths attracted to the light through an open window. I observe them flitting about and, instead of savouring the beauty of their sounds, their sparkling wings and beautiful forms, imbued with feelings of yearning for my distant country and mother tongue, I entice them like a sly predatory hunter.

I don't think there's any connection between the location of my new home and this unavoidable change in my understanding of being a writer. Or rather I didn't think that, until curiosity drove me to do some research on the history of this street and the origins of its name. I had previously lived in two-roomed attics in similar districts of Paris, where I would sit at my table in front of scattered sheets of blank paper, looking out of the window at cloudy skies, damp walls, and television aerials standing erect like scarecrows in a field. I see more or less the same view from my new place. However, the Hôtel de Sens, with its towers rising as high as my attic room, has introduced a different flavour to the scene. I just can't keep my eyes off its courtyard and high surrounding walls. Whenever I sit down to write, the words that gather on the blank paper in front of me refuse to form into proper structures. Instead, I see them scatter and fly out towards the courtyard of Hôtel de Sens which, with its turrets, towers, crenellations and entrance gate that still bears the marks of a drawbridge, is more reminiscent of a medieval chateau than the usual 'Hôtel Particulier'[16] found in this old quarter of Paris. What can I do? I can't control the words; I'm unable to discipline them as I did before. If I manage to catch any and pin them to the page, others manage to escape. Previously, there was a sort of pact between us. Their captivity was linked to my freedom as a writer. Until recently, I've written my books by harnessing words, moving them around in accordance with the rules of grammar, pulling them into shape – you might almost say I was training them. They were not so unruly before, even when I was struggling with grammar to find new ways of expression. Words were under my control. So were letters. Letters never did what they're doing now, which is breaking away from one word and attaching themselves to another; they infuriate me with their acrobatic tricks and total disregard for the meanings I try to convey. Now, when I want to write, they escape my grasp and take on a life of their own. The more I try to constrain them, the more rebellious and defiant they become. The pact between us, or the bond stemming from the master/slave relationship, has turned into some sort of strange game. While in the eyes of the reader I'm a respected author, I've become a pitiable victim of this game. For instance, when writing the title of this story, it would never have occurred to me that a 'z' might escape

16. Urban mansion, typically separated from the street by a courtyard.

from the beginning of one word and land in front of the 'i' of another. But that's what happened. Somehow, the title *Incirli Kuyu*[17] had turned into *Zincirli Kuyu*[18]. The letters had simply ignored my wishes. Whether I liked it or not, I had to change the story to accommodate them. Then words started to break out of their sentences. Words, which have been out of my control ever since I moved to rue du Figuier, surfaced like bubbles in water and, despite all my efforts, flew over to the Hôtel de Sens. At first, I thought this flight was due to the strange name of the building, which might be translated into Turkish as *Anlamlar Oteli*.[19] And why not? A meaningful name like that could be attractive to them. The Hôtel de Sens seemed to exist in another world; I trembled at the thought of winds of the Middle Ages still blowing through its dark corridors. It was named after the Archbishop Salazar of Sens, for whom it was built, and it was now seducing my beloved words away, words produced for my readers with such effort from the recesses of my memory and the most sensitive corners of my heart. But how was I to know there was a dry well in its courtyard?

That day, I worked late in the library. French aristocratic families had lived in the Hôtel de Sens since the sixteenth century, but it was now being used as a library. That building, which had harboured countless mysteries, passions, intrigues and frightful crimes, now housed thousands of books. The grand hall had once hosted balls at which aristocrats would laugh and enjoy themselves, dancing in the flickering light of the wood-burning fire; whereas now there were just a few bibliophiles like me, reading and working, totally oblivious of the darkness falling outside the stained-glass window.

That day, I had stayed late at the library, completely forgetting about the Paris evening that suddenly descends on the city's roofs. I was startled by a hand on my shoulder.

17. Fig Tree Well.
18. Well of Chains
19. 'Hotel of Senses' or 'Hotel of Meanings'.

It was the library warden. He said that it was past closing time; he had not disturbed me until then because I was so engrossed in my book, but now it was time to leave. If I wished, I could borrow the book and take it home. I thanked him for his thoughtfulness and went out carrying the book. As I was going down the steps, he shouted after me, 'The watchman's already shut the main door. You can go through the courtyard and out of the back door.'

I had no idea that the Hôtel de Sens had any doors other than the entrance where the drawbridge used to be. So as not to trouble the warden further, I didn't ask where the back door was. I went quickly down the steps and into the courtyard. It was now evening and had become very dark. Yellow light was shining from the window of the main hall onto the courtyard. I turned towards the light and, looking up, saw the warden watching me. For a moment, our eyes met. Then, just as I was about to make a gesture asking the way, the light suddenly went out. I was left in darkness. The streetlight did not reach over the high walls into the courtyard. I decided to go back into the library and find the warden so that I could leave the building with him. However, just as I was about to turn back, he appeared behind me and shone the torch into the darkest corner of the courtyard.

'Through there, sir,' he whispered in my ear, 'Through the door at the bottom of Fig Tree Well.'

There was neither a fig tree nor a well in sight. The torchlight skimmed over the thick stone walls of the courtyard and lit up the concrete floor. Seeing me hesitate, he said, 'I understand your apprehension, sir. Despite the fact that you come here regularly, you clearly don't know the history of this building that's now our library.'

'Until recently, I didn't. That's true. But I read in the book you gave me that the Hôtel de Sens was built in the sixteenth century for Archbishop Salazar of Sens.'

'I'm talking about the ancient history of the building, sir. If you look at the address on your library card, you'll see that you live in the next street. At number four, rue du Figuier.[20] Your understanding of history appears to be restricted to a few centuries. Haven't you ever wondered about the origin of the name of the street where you live?'

I didn't have time to spend chatting with the warden. I wanted to leave and get home as quickly as possible. However, he had been kind to me, so I tried not to appear impolite.

'If I wasn't curious, I wouldn't have come here and asked you for *Paris Streets*. Unfortunately, I didn't find any information about rue du Figuier that went further back than the sixteenth century. It must be the same age as the Hôtel de Sens.'

'If you look at the records, that's what you'll see. But I know that many years before the Hôtel de Sens was built, when this district did not yet exist and Paris consisted of a city called Lutèce with a population of twenty thousand, a fig tree stood where this street is. Yes, as far back as that. Later, a well was dug out beside the tree, which had been planted there to provide shade for people to cool down and relax in. In those days, this area was used for growing vegetables, and the well was made for gardeners to water their crops. The well is still there. The fig tree withered and disappeared long ago but, when the Hôtel de Sens was being built, they mixed the mortar with water drawn from Fig Tree Well. They say Queen Margo used to have her lovers killed and thrown down this well after using them for a single night of passion.'

I'd started to become impatient. None of this really interested me.

'Excuse me,' I said, 'I need to be somewhere very soon. Can we discuss this tomorrow? I'll come again tomorrow. Let's go now.'

'I understand your rush, sir. However, please don't ignore what I am telling you. Whether or not we can get out

20. Fig tree

of here depends on Fig Tree Well.'

'I don't understand. You just said I could go out by the back door.'

'Yes, but to reach the back door we have to go down into the well. The door I mentioned isn't here. It's in the inner courtyard.'

'What do you mean?' I asked uncertainly. 'Look, I live on the top floor of the building opposite. From there, I can see every part of the Hôtel de Sens. I'd definitely have noticed if there was another inner courtyard, as well as this one.'

'I know how you spend your nights writing by the light of the lamp, how you keep raising your head from the blank paper in front of you and looking into the Hôtel de Sens courtyard. I've been monitoring you ever since you moved in there. You know, you can't learn everything by just looking down from above.'

'What do you mean? I've examined all the old documents in the archives and there's no such courtyard in even the most detailed plans of the building. You're clearly imagining things.'

He didn't answer but just smiled in a rather pedantic manner. I was losing patience.

'Let's get out of here straight away,' I insisted.

'You can't leave straight away.'

'Why?'

'We have to go down into Fig Tree Well first.'

He told me to follow him and started walking. We made our way to the far end of the courtyard and stopped. He shone the torch onto one of the moss-covered stones in the wall, and said, 'We go this way.'

In the light, I saw the stone move. A space opened up that was just wide enough for one person to squeeze through. He went through first and held the torch to show me the way. I went through the space and found myself in in a dark, narrow corridor. Bending almost double, we walked to an inner courtyard. In the middle of this secret courtyard, which I guessed was surrounded by the internal walls of one of the towers, there was a well. We walked towards the well. He started climbing down a rope ladder that hung down inside the well. I followed. For some reason, I was not feeling the slightest bit frightened. I had no apprehensions whatsoever. Everything seemed very natural. I hadn't noticed how the time had passed while reading about rue du Figuier in the library, and my conversation with the warden, my following him and coming out into this secret courtyard, my going down a rope ladder into a dried-up well – this all seemed quite normal. As if it was my usual route when I returned home in the evening to sit at my writing table. The pedantic talk of the warden, the beetles scurrying away in the torchlight, the spiders' webs that stuck to my legs as I descended - I found none of it strange. We finally reached the bottom of the well. In front of us was a dark high-ceilinged corridor which we were able to pass down with ease. We walked for a long time, past walls oozing with water. As we walked, a sound of chains grew closer. We stopped in front of an iron door. The warden knocked on the door. The rusty door creaked open and I found myself dazzled by light. We were in a very large cellar which was lit by projectors. Men in uniforms were moving about. As my eyes grew accustomed to the projectors, I saw a pile of books in the middle of the cellar floor. The uniforms were selecting books from the pile and carrying them to steel shelves that ran from floor to ceiling in the cellar. When the shelves were full, they were chained from both ends.

'Here we are in the Well of Chains,' said the warden. 'Please, hide the book you've just borrowed. If the uniforms see it, they'll chain that one up too.'

I hid the book in the inside pocket of my jacket. We walked along in front of the shelves. Nobody took any interest in us. They were busy collecting books that were being thrown down from above into the middle area, putting them on the shelves and chaining them up.

'These are books which have been censored by the government,' continued the warden. 'Don't worry about how many there are. If you counted them all up, there'd be no more than a hundred. But when a book is banned, all editions are taken off the market. They're brought here and chained up. Sometimes the authorities summon me to help them draw up lists.'

So the warden was really an informer. This two-faced pedant made his living from books; he handed out books to readers during the day and prepared lists of books to be banned at night.

'How can you do such a despicable thing?' I yelled.

'Don't get cross with me,' he said mockingly, 'I adore books. I'm mad about books. I love them and I beat them. They're like my children.'

'But you don't have to educate books!'

'Why not? They're born, grow and go their own way, right or wrong, just like people. And then, sir, they die and disappear. Their pages decompose in the earth, like corpses.'

'No! Books don't die. People die, but books never die!'

'Some of them die even before they're born. Like yours.'

'Like mine?'

'Yes. There are books of yours chained up here: some died before they could be born, others died at birth. But you don't even know it.'

I was stunned by what the warden said. The Turkish courts had just revoked the government ban on my books. So what was he trying to say? Seeing me looking at him in astonishment, he stopped one of the uniforms and told him to put down the books he was carrying. The uniform immediately put down the books, as if the order had come from a superior. He stood to attention, saluted and moved away. The warden picked up a book from the pile on the floor and handed it to me.

'Here, this is your latest book.'

I was startled to see my name on the front cover. It carried the title of a collection of stories that I had planned to write but had never managed to complete. It was a nicely bound edition. I flicked through it and was filled with horror. They were the stories I had been struggling to write since moving to rue du Figuier.

'This was a graveyard for unwritten books long before the military regime was proclaimed,' said the warden. 'Now censored books have got mixed up with them. You have books here in both categories. Ever since the ban on your books was revoked by those liberal-minded judges, your unwritten books have multiplied. Therefore, one might say that you're censoring them yourself. As for me, I'm just doing my job. I like writers, actually. If you want to continue writing, you should move away from here as soon as possible. Leave those defiant, rebellious words to their own devices. Although, even if you do get away from rue du Figuier, they'll still make for the light of your lamp and find you.'

I felt a sudden unbearable desire to leave that damned graveyard. The detestable so-called library warden was in truth a graveyard warden. Not even a graveyard warden, but a loathsome grave robber! I didn't let him accompany me as far as the door. I moved away from him quickly and began running after my words, which were flying back to the Hôtel de Sens courtyard. As I emerged through the rusty iron door, which creaked shut behind me, I decided to write about how the intended title of my latest story, *Incirli Kuyu,* came to be *Zincirli Kuyu.* I continued running, followed by the sound of chains; the dark, damp walls of the corridor seemed to shudder, as if the book-laden shelves were collapsing behind me.

# La Pieta

No city sounds fill the room when he opens the window. Rome is silent. This time, Rome consists of a dark, stone courtyard. At its centre stands a marble fountain. In the dim light, blocked by high rectangular buildings, the water is like a distant dream at the end of a sleepless night. It pours from a mermaid's mouth into a pool. At the bottom of the pool are some mossy pebbles and a few motionless fish. The dappled sides of the fish gleam. Water is slowly eroding the mouth of the reclining mermaid, who faces an array of old furniture left out on rear balconies.

He wonders how a flow of water can be so clear and silent in a secluded courtyard that hardly sees the light of day. Not a sound is to be heard. The flowers in the row of pots next to the pool have withered. The courtyard is covered with pigeon droppings. For a while, he lets his gaze wander over the damp stone walls and the closed window shutters. Everyone must be sleeping. Luxuriating in that morning sleep when memories seem to be enveloped by dark waters.

He closes the wooden shutters, taking care not to make a noise, and returns to his bed, leaving the window open. He sinks into the cool of the sheets in which he has tossed and turned all night. Rome is silent.

This time, Rome consists of a barely discernible memory of a past journey, and of a sad lonely body slipping into damp sheets waiting for sleep – his body.

A woman's voice, which seems close, yet is very distant; a face that is somehow always the same face; the impassioned tautness of a body in a hotel room. A naked body, tensed in a paroxysm of love-making.

The voice says, 'Come, die in my arms!' She was bending over him, looking at him gently, lovingly. As if to protect him from the darkness of the night, from the dizzying emptiness of the deep, windy stormy chasm opening before him.

'I need you so much,' she says. 'One more time. Please, one more time.' The body tenses like an arched bow. He decides that the cry of 'Come, die in my arms' must be just the wail of a wild cat climbing the tiles of a roof in the light of a full moon. He slackens and collapses.

'One last time,' says the voice. 'One last time.' The face looks sadly at his naked, deflated body, cringing on the bed. It is a face with the tenderness of a twenty year-old girl. The woman sits astride his wilting body, which starts to stir and revive as she begins to move. 'Be hard inside me, stay like that!' she says. 'Strong and hard - forever!' Her slender-fingered hands wrap around his neck and her panting gradually subsides. Once again, he tenses with sorrow. The cries of the wildcat are no longer to be heard. Rome is silent.

That time, when they were here together, city sounds had filled the room when he opened the window. The roar of buses, horns, brakes, people's voices, calls... the bells of St Agnese. It had never occurred to him that a hotel near Piazza Navona, in this small cobbled street, with its old orange-coloured houses, could be so noisy. There had been nothing alien about the crowds at the station terminal when they alighted from the Paris train. They had drunk their coffee at a little bar opposite the platforms where trains were waiting to set off for southern cities with narrow white streets, or to the north for hazy evenings in Milan, or a sunset in Venice's Piazza di San Marco.

After a long night's journey, spent hand in hand, heads together, without talking, it was good to reach Rome and take in the intense aroma and bitter taste of an espresso at a little round table lit by the morning sun. Especially in the company of a young, concupiscent woman who gave more than she took, and was inclined to test his vigour to the limit. Glass panels with scenes of Rome were hung on the walls for the benefit of tourists: the ruins of the Forum, round marble columns and the arched galleries of the Coliseum; the magical play of light on the statues and water in the Trevi Fountain. Another panel showed the dome of the Basilica di San Pietro and the square filled with crowds. It had been exciting to taste the reality of a legendary city, of the 'eternal' Rome, which for centuries had been the centre of the world, and to think about all the ruins and monuments, the museums and churches, and the secrets of corridors and underground mausoleums that they would discover together.

Now he thinks of how the young woman, who sat silently with him in the August heat, would suddenly start talking in the darkness of their shuttered hotel room. It seemed as if the mysteries of this ancient city could be unravelled by the words of that strange, passionate intense woman, who had remained silent ever since they met just one week earlier in Paris. They had taken a taxi and driven through the city's noisy streets and round its sunny squares before reaching the hotels near Piazza Navona, where they had gazed in amazement at the crowds of chattering Italians in the café terraces. The silky, intricate web of soft silence they had spun between Paris and Rome had brought them close together.

Now, he lies on the bed, alone in the room, waiting for time to pass. He arrived in Rome late last night and will fly south to Palermo this evening. A long day lies ahead. As long and futile as his naked body wrapped in sheets that have become damp with perspiration. If he dressed and went out straight away, he could wander round the city until it was time for his flight. He could look out for any changes that have taken place since his previous visit. Or he could go through the familiar streets that led to the Vatican. But first, a coffee on the terrace opposite the Fountain of Four

Rivers in Piazza Navona before the August sun becomes too scorching hot. Then, he could walk among the pigeons and the phaetons awaiting tourists, and go along Vittorio Emanuele II Street to the shores of the Tiber. From there, even if it took longer, he could cross the St Angelo Bridge, with its white statues gleaming in the sunshine, to Piazza di San Pietro. Or he could walk from Piazza Navona away from the Tiber, through the cool cobbled streets to the Trevi Fountain and come out into Piazza di Spagna. And at the far end of the square he could go up the steps to Trinità dei Monti Church. There would be nobody in the church at this early hour of the morning. Jesus would be there alone on the cross. His body as light as a feather in Mary's arms. In the quivering candlelight, Jesus would be there, both on the cross and in the arms of Mary who gave him life. Street sellers would not yet have spread out their trinkets, souvenirs and ivory statues on the steps. He could go past the Trinità dei Monti's two bell towers, like identical twins except that the one on the left is an hour ahead, and up to Villa Borghese Park. From Villa Borghese, the view of Rome, with its red roofs, its earth-coloured stone buildings, its shadowy streets opening into crowded treeless squares and its cool fountains, has a calming effect on people. In the distance, just beyond the tree-lined banks of the Tiber, is the dome of the Basilica di San Pietro, looking like a guardian of the ancient city.

But this time, Rome is not saying much to him. The ruins, stones and fountains are silent. Like the woman he was with the first time he came to this city. They had come to this hotel then as well, and booked into one of the large rooms overlooking the street. But now, he is alone in a small room overlooking the rear courtyard, lying naked on a single bed. He feels no desire at all to go out into the sunny squares and mingle with the crowds, or to wander through the city's familiar streets and revisit museums or monuments.

All he desires is sleep. He just wants to sleep, and to never wake up in this secluded hotel room, where not even the sound of water pouring from the mermaid's mouth in the courtyard can be heard. It is as if he has reached the end of a journey of no return. He had set off on a journey through the loneliness of hotel rooms and single beds, like a ship that gradually leaves the shore behind and becomes caught up in a whirling vortex of unknown seas. A ship driven by the waters of the four large rivers that gush from the statues beneath the obelisk at the centre of Piazza Navona. It goes through fiery African deserts to the Mediterranean Sea and on towards the Nile delta. It weighs anchor in the sacred waters of the mud-coloured Ganges. It makes its way along the Rio de la Plata through herds of cattle on the vast plains of Argentina. Its corroded hull is swept along by the waters of the Danube, which turn out to be not blue at all. It is steered between fields of corn towards the shores of the Black Sea. To the choppy waters of the Black Sea. Suddenly, for some reason the words of an old Turkish song come to mind: *The Danube does not want to flow.* Is it possible for the Danube to stop flowing? Years have passed since squares filled with people singing that song. How much water and how many rivers have passed beneath its bridges? Every decade *The Danube does not want to flow* comes round again. Yet the muddy waters of the Danube keep on flowing over its thousand year-old bed.

As they sipped their coffees in the cafés on the terrace in front of the Fountain of Four Rivers in Piazza Navona, he had wanted to explain everything to the young woman sitting beside him. About how the Danube came to stop flowing, how every time this song was played on the radio before the news was read by a severe and decisive voice, young people, intellectuals, workers' leaders would be rounded up from their homes and taken away; and how on a September day at dawn, when the Danube was no longer flowing on the radio, the woman he loved had died under interrogation.

'Come, die in my arms!' The slender-fingered hands wrap themselves fervently around his neck.

The woman says nothing while they wander all day, hand in hand, under the scorching August sun among the two-thousand year-old stones and columns on the tiers of the Coliseum, where once gladiators fought for their lives in rivers of blood, and docile Christians were tossed as food to the lions. She exhibits not the slightest wonder at the Vatican, or even the intricacies of the Sistine Chapel ceiling where Michelangelo's colours take flight, turning God's beard white and Adam's lifeless fingers brown. Yet at the point when humans are banished from Paradise and devils from the realms of angels, when the land, sky and seas are created with all their living creatures, she reaches out as if embracing the apple tree with her serpentine arms and begins to speak. At first, they are not words, but merely a means of extinguishing the fire within. She bites the man's source of strength as if biting into an apple. As she wraps her hands around his neck, her lithe body makes the man, pulsating beneath her, rise to a climax.

For some reason, he had felt like talking to that woman about the pain he had buried deep inside him during all his years of exile and of which, until that day, he had spoken to no-one. It was morning in Piazza Navona, after a night of feeding their raw desires. They were alone on the sunny terrace. The square had not yet filled with crowds of tourists. A pigeon was perched on the head of one of the long-haired, bearded statues in the Fountain of Four Rivers. He remembers how, with a single flap of its wings, the pigeon had flown away from the head of the statue whose arms stretched forward as if to support the walls of the church of St Agnese, diagonally across the fountain's pool to alight on the cobbles of the square, before perching on the table at which they were sitting. A gentle feeling, that he was unable to identify, made him shiver. A feeling that was reflected from pigeons' wet wings sparkling in the morning sun, a feeling that embraced his whole being.

He had not experienced real love or satisfaction. If

death meant silence, not speaking even when she felt the warmth of the man she loved inside her at night, in the deep hollow of their bed, then he had wanted to tell this woman next to him about his love for someone who had uttered not a word or cry ever since she died under interrogation one September morning. About her creamy skin, her gentleness and loving eyes. About his twenty years of wild living. About his pleasure at the flap of a pigeon's wing.

He wanted to tell the woman sitting next to him that, years ago in Istanbul, he had fallen in love with a university student with whom he had never slept, and about the death under interrogation of this lover who still made him shiver when he dreamt of her touch. About how, under a dazzling light, she had responded to the punches on her tender young face and the torrent of questions by saying, 'I don't know.'

'No!' she had insisted. 'I won't tell you! Even if you kill me, I won't tell you anything!' And, as the bloodstains spread across the floor, the eternal silence of a slender mouth with its jaws clamped shut.

He remembers their last meeting, at Çinaralti Café in Beyazit. The horse chestnut tree under which they were sitting had not yet started to shed its leaves. It was early September. A beautiful, sunny day. The sound of water came from the mosque courtyard. Despite the crowds that filled the cafés, pigeons were coming up to the tables before flying up through the branches of the horse chestnut to the dome of the mosque. His lover talked to him continuously. She was telling him about her childhood days in the countryside, about her brothers, and about the stifling dormitory at the Çemberlitas Student Hostel for Girls. The words had gone in one ear and out the other, leaving no trace, not a single thing in his memory. Her talk was like the continuously flowing water in the mosque courtyard. Clear and monotone. When his lover spoke, a pleasing coolness spread inside him. He felt an irrepressible desire to take her in his arms and kiss her slender moving lips. It was early evening and their table at Çinaralti Café gave them a view of students going in and out of Beyazit Library carrying textbooks, and youngsters heading off to Sahaflar Book Market. His lover used to tell him everything, all about the books she read, the films she saw, the actions she participated in, so there was no way he could have known that, a few days later, she would remain silent at the cost of her life, that not a word would fall from her mouth, and that, according to testimonies made in court by her friends, when electric shocks were applied to her nipples, temples and tongue - that lovely little tongue - she would refuse to talk, or that she would never talk again. After all, the girl who had been with him that evening was just a provincial girl in her twenties. An impulsive girl, exuberant with youth and unlived love. She was caught up in the urgency of those September days.

In Piazza Navona, he wanted to tell the woman, who sat silent as a sphinx opposite him, that silence was not such a great virtue, that although they say 'words may be silver, but silence is golden' about someone who keeps their mouth zipped, it is no justification for dipping the gold into a sea of aqua regia. For some reason, he said nothing. Words that were on the tip of his tongue seemed to get stuck on his lips and, lost in the darkness, they rolled back into the cavity of his mouth. The silence between them that had started on the first day of their journey continued to spin its web.

He muses on how, in Paris, when he received the dreadful news of friends dying under torture, he had not even thought about his first love, yet he had remembered her that morning when a damp-winged pigeon took flight in Piazza Navona. He thinks how, so many years later, the pain had suddenly erupted and enveloped his whole being on that journey, and how it had made him even closer to the woman with him. To be silent or to speak. That was the whole question.

At night in the hotel, the woman, as if compensating for the words of love she did not utter, had wrapped her slender fingers around his neck in order to arouse him one more time, to make him stiffen in her body, which was spread-eagled on the hotel room bed. When she cried out, 'Come, die in my arms!' her words were referring to a love, an unfulfilled passion, which ended years ago on a September morning when the tanks made their way through the empty streets of the city. He knows that now.

This second trip to Rome will have no significance in his life, as it continues on its way like an abandoned ship. This time, Rome consists of a hotel room with closed shutters. This time Rome is silent. He knows now that neither stones nor people will ever speak again. Even the water will be silent. The amnesic water will flow over its riverbed, forgetting those who surrendered their lives under interrogation.

# A Mediterranean Face

DAWN IN A silent courtyard surrounded by high walls. A collar of death. An iron collar that gradually tightens. How it squeezes the slender neck of the condemned man. The executioner leans over the prisoner, whose hands are tied to a stake behind him and, with each breath, tightens the screw of the iron ring a little more. He monitors how, under his expert hands, death is spreading through the prisoner's body at each crack of the cervical vertebrae. How close death is! As if death is in his own fingers, rather than in the cold metal of the collar. As if the executioner is infusing the condemned man with death. The prisoner's face looks deathly white in the light shining from an iron-barred window, as if his dark, youthful face has suddenly turned ashen. His cheeks are hollow, his brow furrowed with pain. There is no-one else in the courtyard. No prosecutor, no officials, no lawyer and no crowds. The executioner and prisoner are alone in the morning frost; the executioner stands close to the prisoner, so close that he could suffocate him without the iron collar. Before bending down to pick up the black cloth lying on the ground, he gives the screw a final twist. He waits for the cervical vertebrae to crack. He hears nothing. Stepping back from the prisoner's body, which has slipped down the stake, he picks up the black cloth. Then, as if there were a crowd needing to be dispersed and official observers of the execution needing to go back to work, or as if those who saw the sorrow on the face of the prisoner, with his staring eyes and protruding tongue, might grasp the true nature of the government with its brutal garrotting of thousands since the inquisition, he picks up the black cloth and places it on the prisoner's head with a matador-like flourish. Above, the sky slowly lights up the high walls surrounding the prison courtyard. A pigeon flies away from one of the iron-barred windows.

He is sitting in Plaza Real, looking at the pigeons. With one flap of their wings, they rise up into the palm trees from the water pipe in the pool at the centre of the square. Unable to find a branch to perch on among the sharp, withered leaves, they return to the pool. Overweight, lazy pigeons. They stroll among the crowds of tourists and the adolescents and vagrants lolling on the benches in the square; rather than peck at crumbs, they opt to cool off in the cloudy water of the pool where, with an occasional shake of their gleaming wings, they make advances to each other in the sunshine. Some of them strut up to empty tables in a military manner. Their mating calls mingle with the sounds of the café.

He thinks of the bird market he has just seen in Las Ramblas. Captive birds in cages. But in his mind, he sees another pigeon, quite different from these obese creatures that are such a part of daily life in the pools and squares of the city. He recalls a pure white pigeon flying from one of the iron-barred windows and landing in a prison courtyard. The flapping of the pigeon's wings seems to emphasise the silence of the courtyard at dawn. Far away, beyond the high walls, the clapper of a church bell swings in vain. A heavy, rusty clapper, moving like a pendulum from right to left and left to right. There is no sound in the church. The streets are deserted, the windows dark. Suddenly, an awesome sound is heard as the clapper touches the inside of the bell. The ancient walls reverberate as if lightning has struck the bell tower. Metallic, rasping sounds echo from the roofs of the houses into the courtyard. The pigeon takes flight immediately. Darting from one wall to another, from the concrete courtyard to the gallows. How its frightened red-rimmed eyes sparkle! How white its slender neck and lean body! It flies over the wall in the morning darkness, leaving a few feathers on the black cloth covering the head of the bound prisoner.

This is a magnificent square that lives up to its name, with its cafés and restaurants beneath arched galleries. From where he is sitting, he can see the yellow walls of three-storey buildings, pots of flowers lined up on balconies, the interiors of high-ceilinged rooms and, a little beyond, the glow of sun-tanned young couples embracing in the shade of palm trees. Everything is so close. The burning of the sun, human friendship. As if the world has been purged of all its filth. In the light, the hum of Las Ramblas and the roar of double-decker buses in the nearby streets mingle and echo through the stone arches around the square.

He had arrived in Barcelona at dawn that morning. As soon as he arrived, he left his case at a hotel in Plaza Cataluña and went out to mingle with the crowds. He walked under the plane trees in La Rambla and down to the harbour. Weaving among red and green birds, parrots and canaries, water-sellers, long-eared tawny rabbits, tanks of multi-coloured fish. Barcelona was a like fairground, enticing him with the magical gaiety of its pigeons, bird markets and flower shops. He walked in the shade of plane trees, in front of cafés, newspaper vendors and displays of books. With each step, he felt the excitement of discovering a new city and feeling its pulse; it was like touching the body of a woman for the first time. The narrow streets that cut across the main road twisted and turned towards the old quarters, where they wound between gothic buildings and stone walls towards the harbour. He went straight down the main road without turning off into any of the side streets.

When he arrived at the harbour, he felt tired. He sat on a bench in front of the *Colon,* where Christopher Columbus watches over the ships setting out to sea. Everything had its own colour, its own reality. The white passenger ships, the colourful motorboats, the Mediterranean sun, which looked ready to explode in the sky at any moment. Also the birds, the trees and the humid heat. The model of the Santa Maria that took Columbus to America was shoddily constructed, just as it had been hundreds of years ago. After a sleepless train journey, he loved the morning tranquillity of the sea, even in a noisy port. For years, he had been living far from the sea among the stone and concrete piles of a European city. In an incongruous district of old buildings surrounded by skyscrapers. Whenever he saw the sea, it aroused the same yearning, the same feelings in him. To return… To be able to return to the sandy beaches of his childhood and adolescence, to that white city on the shores of the Mediterranean…

The days were fading and disappearing among his things on the wall of a dusty room, between the Koran and the gilded 'Bismillahirrahmanirrahim'[21]. As his mother waited, the days were fragmenting and disintegrating; the dark, smiling Mediterranean face on the wall was losing its vigour. Yet faces remain the same age forever, in photographs. However, he knew that after years of moving from one city to another, one hotel to another, his face had aged, even in the photograph on the wall of that distant home; it had become the face of an exile without identity. The days of the past came flooding back, reviving forgotten school books in the box room and photos on the wall, like the quickening of the earth after sudden torrents of rain. Pages became wet and soggy, writing illegible, eyes blurred.

The face in that photograph was now looking at ships anchored in Barcelona harbour. But his smile and freshness had long since disappeared, lost in the anonymity of crowds. The eyes which looked down from the wall at his mother when she performed her early morning prayers, at the cat sleeping on the divan, were not the eyes that looked out to sea in this foreign port.

He rose from the bench and walked the length of the

---

21. 'In the name of God, the Lord of Mercy, the Giver of Mercy' — *The Qur'an : A new translation by M. A. S. Abdel Halleem*, p. 3, Oxford World Classics, 2010.

quay. He spent a long time looking at some shearwaters, twirling and hovering in the air. He thought of the storks coming over the Toros Mountains, after days of flying across the plain, and landing on the beach with downy, exhausted wings. One of them had built a nest in their chimney and broken the radio aerial. His mother had said that it was a great sin to destroy the nest of a stork on its way to Mecca, so he had stopped listening to radio music and devoted himself entirely to books. That was when it all started. The high school adolescent, whose only preoccupations had been listening to radio music and day-dreaming, vanished and was replaced by a dark, handsome young man. That summer, he had left home at the same time as the stork, which abandoned the chimney never to return. He didn't exactly join a sect, but he did become involved with some young activists.

The sea was no longer calm. It was rekindling old wounds and reminding him of his nomadic days. On a whim, he turned round and walked away from the quay and down one of the side streets. Maybe by the time he reached Plaza Real, he would be able to throw off the escalating feelings that at any moment might turn to melancholy. He tried to think about the Spanish Civil War, those bloody days when Franco's soldiers marched on Plaza Cataluña, and about the extraordinary resistance of the Republicans.

But now, as he sits in a café in Plaza Real, he does not think about the Barcelona of fifty years ago. He pushes aside the image of that fluttering white pigeon. He does not want to remember the existence of his mother, who waits with increasing optimism, completing her reading of the Koran and renewing her vows each year. At this moment, only Spain is in his mind. Memories of his first trip to Spain.

They had travelled across the country in one day, from the north to the southwest. They were two people in an old car. Having vowed never to set foot on Spanish soil while Franco lived, they had driven non-stop to the Portuguese border. In the spring of 1974, they were going to Lisbon, the city of the 'Carnation Revolution'. He remembers the earth-coloured churches, the fields of wheat, the scattered gardens and snow-capped peaks. For him, Spain consisted of these images, as well as the paintings of Goya and the poems of Lorca and Rafael Alberti. Naturally, they could not have known that their fascination with the Spanish towns, through which they passed without stopping, the guest houses in which they never stayed, the ruined towers on mountainsides, this forbidden world which flew past outside the window, would be transformed into a nightmare within a fortnight. How was he to know that, by not setting foot on Spanish soil, not spending even a day in Madrid or Toledo or getting a proper taste of the country, his impressions of Spain would be obliterated from his memory! Their return from Lisbon, and the brutality he saw in a newspaper one morning, had suddenly dispelled any desire for travel. For a long, long time after that, Spain would conjure up images of staring eyes and a tongue protruding from an ashen face. The face of Puig Antich of the Iberian Resistance Movement, who was condemned to suffocation by the Spanish garrotte early one morning in 1974 in the courtyard of Barcelona Prison. In the cold of the iron collar, that face had been suffused with death by the hand of the executioner. That face, once so full of life, with kindly eyes, was the face of a young man of twenty-six.

He did not devote much time to the memory of Puig. The night was spent lovemaking and, towards dawn, sleeping. Yet something of Puig seemed to permeate every animate object, every living body that he touched. Life was a continuation of Puig's world. Kernels of news about blood and violence, to which he became a little more inured every day, had continued to tumble out of newspaper pages, television screens, telex machines. Now, as he sits in Puig's city, in a sunny Barcelona café sipping a beer, he thinks of his past. A Mediterranean face comes to mind, a face that winces more each time the executioner tightens the screw. The ashen face with the bulging eyes must have grown up in an environment similar to that of the dark, smiling face in the photograph on the wall of that remote house, must have looked at similar seas and skies. Who knows, maybe their fate was determined by a similar stork's nest. Neither of those faces exists now. One lost to the cruelty of the executioner, the other to oblivion on the wheel of time.

Soon, he will get up from his chair. He will eat alone in a crowded restaurant before his midday sleep. He will not share with anybody, not even the young people around him, the joy of setting foot in a Spain that embraced freedom fifty years ago. This joy is of little significance for them. It is a happiness that stems from his own past and his current exile, which only nomads like himself can comprehend. Back at the hotel, he will not look in the mirror when he gets into a bath to shed some of the fatigue of his journey; not the sleepless night-time journey, but the journey of no return that goes on for years. But there is still time before his midday sleep. The sun is not yet overhead. Plaza Real is humming, the cafés are crowded. His face is reflected in the lens of a tourist taking pictures of the pigeons by the pool. A pigeon flutters its damp wings. Just as the shutter is released, it flies out of the frame with unexpected speed for its fat body. All that remains in the photograph is a few feathers and an abstracted face in the background, looking at the square with the eyes of a stranger.

# Last Summer

THEY WERE LIKE two foreigners in their own country. Nights spent sipping iced whiskies in a bar, daytimes running from one museum to another, sunset on the quay, sunrise in Bosphorus cafés, and mornings in the choppy seas of their bed. When they awoke the world was turning blue. The 7:15 ferry passed through their bedroom every morning, like a familiar guest. It was the first ferry, taking working people and apprentices from the shacks on the slopes of Anadoluhisari to Eminönü and to the dark workshops of Bakircilar Çarsi and Çagaloglu. Every morning, they were framed in the gilded Venetian mirror next to the walnut console table. Wrapped in light reflected from sunlit waters. By the time the 9.20 ferry was approaching the quay, the tea was brewed. They took breakfast in the garden, opposite Rumelihisari. White cheese, olives, rose marmalade… Things untouched by alien hands.

The sun would shine down on the waters beneath the Hisar fortifications, illuminating the towers, bastions and castle walls. The 9:20 ferry would pass by, almost touching the villa, and then move away with a few smartly dressed passengers, leaving a white foamy wash behind. Of course, their past had had its turbulence too. Memories and disasters that had been dispersed and lost in the wash of time. But they were young. Life was still waiting to be lived. Within touching distance, like the opposite shore. New delights, untasted passions. The present moment was just the start of an endless summer day. They embarked on it, not with the anxieties of people going to work in the morning, but with a feeling of physical closeness after a night of loving. The city belonged to them. For years, they had been far away from Istanbul. Far from the traffic congestion and crowds of rogues spilling off the pavements, and far from the winter rain and mud. From the over-crowded buses, defective telephones, empty promises and bouncing cheques. They both lived in Europe. For them, on a clear sunny day, when the sea was calm and the mosque courtyards shaded by plane trees, Istanbul was a holiday city. But at the first drop of rain, it was an abandoned city, forgotten like a former lover, banished to oblivion in the tumult of daily life. They had not been apart since they met in a garden bar close to the European side of the Bosphorus Bridge. They went everywhere together. At their friends' villa in Anadoluhisar?, in the streets, on ferry quays, in the mosques and churches which they never tired of wandering around, among the crowds in the market - they were together all the time, everywhere. They made a good pair. Their skins were suntanned, their hair had grown. They knew that their days together were numbered, that the moment the holiday was over they would return to their respective cities, and that they would not see each other for a very long time, maybe never again. It was undoubtedly better that way. They would part before their relationship had become a habit, before they grew to hate each other, before they were forced into any situation. At the end of a beautiful summer of love and passion. But then a telegram arrived one night and the woman suddenly broke off the holiday and went back to work. The man was left on his own. Alone in a vacuum.

*Your sudden departure upset me less than I might have expected. I was left on my own. Alone in a vacuum. No, I didn't feel pain. I hadn't grown so used to you that I felt pain at your departure. You weren't a part of my body. But it was lovely being with you, starting and ending the day with you. You generated in me a feeling that was both comforting and pleasantly frivolous. We had no joint plans for the future. We weren't the sort of couple to put pressure* on each other, to limit each other's freedom, to destroy the desires of love and the pleasures of passion. Our time together was like our separation. Simple, dignified and measured. Actually, there's no need for me to write all this to you. You know and experienced everything with me. If such things mean happiness, I was happy with you. But, your unexpected departure threw me into a vacuum that is difficult to identify, even though I was in some ways prepared for your absence. I became strangely distant from the world. With you, there were familiar faces, friends and sunny days. With you, the Bosphorus was blue, Istanbul eternal. It was you who brought colour to my world, who taught me to love this city that I had left seven years before. So I must have liked you and taken pleasure in your company. An irrational and wild pleasure. The writer, addicted to whirlwinds of desire and pain, inflicted by whips of pleasure, was replaced by a mature man. With you, sex was not merely a part of daily life and existence. It was as natural as sunlight, as real as the water I drank. That's why your departure did not leave me with an open wound. It didn't feel as if a piece of my body had broken away. I didn't have nightmares about your absence. But I found myself in a strange vacuum. My links with the outside world and those around me suddenly shrank. People and things became distant. I never went back to the bar where we drank whisky, where I'd gone alone to meet a woman and where, later, I'd gone to meet her friend. Nor did I go back to the villa at Hisar. I just gathered up my things, thanked the friends who had let us the villa for the summer, and went to my mother's timber house in Yenikapi.

My mother was delighted to see me. I didn't get the usual complaint that when I came to Istanbul I never made time to see her, but spent all my time with shady looking people and foreign women. For once, she looked happy. Every summer since I went abroad, her face had worn the same look of sad reproach when she opened the door to me - a tired-looking stranger. But this time, there was look of softness and affection on her face as well. The way she expected nothing of anyone, certainly no miracles, was reminiscent of the way the Holy Mother Mary understood that the lifeless body in her arms did not belong to her, but was the son of God. At first, *we said nothing. But she'd sensed something. Things that I neither knew nor comprehended. That night, I slept in the living room to the ticking of the chiming clock. In the morning, she laid out breakfast in the back room overlooking the railway. For a very brief moment, I wished I could be with you in Hisar. I wanted to dive with you into the foamy waters behind the 9.20 ferry, to gaze at the streaks of silver in the choppy waters as children on the jetty cried out, 'Bluefish! Bluefish!' To be sipping my tea opposite you. There was a long day ahead of me. I had no idea how I would spend it, on which shore or with whom I would walk, in which café or how I would amuse myself.*

*It started with the summer sun shining on the railway below, and on the fig tree sprouting from the crumbling Byzantine ramparts opposite - a summer sun that was causing unhealed wounds to go septic. I drank my tea quickly so as to make a rapid escape from that house where every room contained ghosts of the past, memories of childhood and unfulfilled adolescent desires. My mother poured me the usual second glass of tea and gestured with her hand for me to remain seated. There was a strange gravity, an uncomfortable silence about her, that I'd never seen before. Down below, the suburban train, crammed with commuters, was slowly grinding towards Sirkeci. The tea glasses on the table and the wooden chair, on which I was sitting, shuddered. My mother, sitting opposite me, swayed with the balcony. I thought how a more severe tremor might cause the floorboards to open up and the walls to come crashing down on me; how two trains passing simultaneously in opposite directions might cause the collapse of this timber house left to us by my mother's grandfather. Death was close at hand. Watching us, waiting for an opportunity. Soon, my mother would say that she'd spent her whole life waiting for me, that it was time I came back, settled down and had a family. The rumbling of the train stopped and the tremors ended.*

*However, contrary to what I'd expected, she didn't say, 'Life is short, but the journey's long.' She said nothing, nothing at all. She just gazed at me intently. Never before had she looked at me so intently, so sadly. I shivered with a feeling of grief that gradually spread through my body, a grief that I had been trying to forget for years. Finally she spoke, rolling her words around her toothless mouth and deliberating over them as if, rather than merely repeating what she said every year, she was saying something new this time, although this had been going on for seven years.*

*'It's visiting day today.' Encouraged by the fact that, for the first time in seven years, I was neither pretending not to hear, nor interrupting her, she continued, 'Go to her this time. Yes, you must definitely go!'*

*No boiling water rained down on me. I didn't jump up in anger as if suppressing some other feeling. For some reason, I felt at ease. It's difficult to explain to you how the feeling of emptiness you left behind had suddenly disappeared, how everything had suddenly become clear in my head.*

*'Okay, but don't come with me,' I said to my mother. 'If the package is ready, give it to me and I'll take it.' She raised her elderly body with surprising agility and ran out to the kitchen. She came back with a large package in her hands. I put the package into a nylon bag and went out.*

*I walked along by the shore for a long time, looking at the sea, the anchored ships and the islands. There were fishing boats by the quay. Seagulls screamed and circled above them. The drone of the city mingled with the sound of lapping water. Seven years had seemingly never passed; time had stood still. It was the Istanbul of seven years ago. The same sea, same shore, same sun. The same excitement inside me, and still the same white cloud up there. I was going to meet my lover, by road and sea. She was waiting for me in a café, with the ever-present books by her side. We were going to talk about the world and the beautiful days to come. Her long wavy hair made me tremble inside. The nightmare days of September had not yet descended over the city. There were no tanks stationed on street corners; the hunting season had not yet begun. Then, as I walked, time started to move on as well. The ticking of the chiming clock that had punctuated my sleep came closer with every step. Years passed. While I had been travelling across the seven seas of the world, Istanbul had grown by seven years. Exactly seven years. I hailed a taxi and told the driver, 'Sagmalcilar Prison.'*

*We went along the city walls towards Yediküle. We drove*

*down bustling streets, through crowds setting off for the beach in the morning sun. Then we turned off into some dark, narrow side streets. I had sunk into the back seat, allowing the wind to blow in my face through the open window. I wasn't thinking of anything; I wasn't missing anyone - not even you. I was just holding on tightly to the nylon bag in my hand. There was one aim in my life, one reason for my existence. To get the package to its destination as soon as possible.*

*She wasn't a bit surprised to see me. We looked at each other for a long time. Time stopped once more. But we weren't sitting hand in hand at Çinaraltı Café. There were seas, mountains, countries between us. We were far apart from each other, yet also closer than ever before. Time began to move forward. Only then did I notice the deep hollows of her eyes on her small, thin face. Only then did I see the furrows on her brow and the loneliness in her eyes. Her hair was as black as ever. But it was dirty and lank. It hung over her shoulders, making her face look even longer. She was wearing the prison uniform issued to all inmates. I handed her the package. She took it straight away and put it to one side without opening it.*

*'Don't you want to see what's inside?'*

*'...'*

*'Hey... How are you?'*

*'I'm fine. And you? Tell me, where have you been?'*

*I finally heard it. After seven years of waiting to be asked, I heard the question from her.*

*'I've been abroad. I didn't stay long in Istanbul after your arrest.'*

*'Yes, I know. Your mother told me everything.'*

*I relaxed. Inside I felt a sea of blue stir inside me. Do mothers ever say bad things? She must have said that of course I hadn't forgotten her, that I always mentioned her in my letters even if I hadn't written to the prison yet, that I hadn't written because I was afraid something bad might happen to her, that I'd been saying how much I missed her for seven years.*

*'Never mind my mother. Don't believe everything she says.'*

*She smiled. An indefinable sorrow spread over her face.*

*'No, no!' she said. 'Mothers always speak the truth.'*

My mother must have told her that I still loved her, that I was waiting for her and we would get married when she came out of prison.

*'You've lost a lot of weight. You must take care of yourself.'*

*'And you, you've grown fat. I guess you probably drink too much. I can tell from the way you write.'*

*'Are you able to read what I write?'*

*'Of course. Magazines and newspapers have been coming in here regularly for the last two years. But no books are allowed in. I'm told they get expurgated and then sold outside. It's forbidden to bring them here. You're on the blacklist.'*

*'And I expect I'm on your blacklist. Are you angry with me?'*

*'I follow your travels through your newspaper articles. I love the way you write about the places you go to and the women you meet.'*

*'Don't tease me. Please don't.'*

*'What makes you think I'm teasing you? I really like your articles. I'm able to travel the world with you. You lift us up. The walls collapse and a patch of blue sky opens above our heads. Thanks to you, we have a breath of fresh air.'*

*'You're going too far now! Anyone would think that it's easy living abroad and getting by in Europe!'*

*'Don't be cross, darling. You have many admirers at the prison. Some girls even cut photos of you out of magazines and pin them up by their beds.'*

*'You haven't changed at all. Your teasing is as brutal as ever. But I don't want to feel guilty any more. Do you understand that? I wish I'd never come.'*

*'It was a good thing you went to Europe. Have you come back for good now?'*

*'No, I'm going again. And I'm never coming back.'*

*'Then it's a good thing you came. We may never see each other again.'*

*I suddenly wanted to embrace her with all my strength, even though I knew her delicate body would crumple and break in my arms like a carefully nurtured hot-house flower. I wanted to press her against my heart. Just then, they announced the end of visiting time. I wanted to yell, as she was being escorted back to the prison ward by two guards; to cry out to the crowd of people on my side of the wire screen, to the stone walls, to the whole of Istanbul, that I loved her just as much as I did seven years ago, even more so. For some reason, no sound came out of my mouth except a muffled squawk. As I write these lines to you, the words break out and turn into twisted letters, fluttering like moths flying into the light of the lamp. Soon they'll attack and suffocate me. After that summer passed, their lies were the only reality in my life. From now on, I can write only for myself, not for you.*

*Forget me, but don't forget last summer!*

# Houses

HE WAS SITTING alone at the bar. In front of a brightly illuminated display of drinks. How close the row of whisky, vodka, gin, cognac and Cointreau bottles was. If he reached out his hand, he could touch every one of them. Lit up like that, they looked like players in a grand orchestra. It wasn't only their colours, but their forms and tastes. Especially tastes. He ordered another whisky on the rocks. The barman knew this type of customer only too well, the type whose drinking accelerated as the night wore on.

'Of course,' he said in English, though there was nothing English about him. He tapped the bar with his fingers, trying to keep time with the music on the cassette player. Then, he slowly took the lid off the ice bucket, put two large lumps of ice into a glass and added a shot of whisky. He set the glass in front of the customer. 'Here you are, sir.'

If he'd spoken in his own language, he would have said, 'Parakola kiryos.' That would have been preferable, but hardly appropriate in the bar of a luxury seaside hotel. Of course the barman was going to say 'Here you are, sir' with that air of indifference, just as he had done the previous night.

The customer had come to this hotel to attend a meeting. He'd heard of it before. The Astir Palace was in Vuliagmeni, a coastal district of Athens. It was odd that he hadn't noticed how, in his own language, the name of the hotel sounded like 'clear off',[22] only ruder. For three days, he'd been speaking to writers from all over the world in French or English, with no qualms about putting in the odd

22. 'Hastir' is a colloquial contraction of 'Ha siktir' – meaning 'fuck off'.

Greek word. For some reason, this place seemed genuine to him. The Greeks loved him, which enhanced his image as a Turkish author in reluctant, self-imposed exile. One day, he really should write about how this neighbouring country was just as hospitable as his own. But suddenly, probably owing to the effect of too much whisky, the name of the hotel made him think of other unplanned commitments. Yes, he must go. He had to clear off, to get away from there, for ever. The following morning he would leave this hotel, this city, at the crack of dawn. He would pack his belongings and f- off.[23]

The hotel was quite a long way from the town centre. You could spend all day in the sea or sunbathing by the pool. No noise intruded from the rumbling vehicles pounding up and down the grid of streets, or from the constantly chattering crowds in the café terraces and treeless squares. By the pool, it was tranquil. The sun was scorching hot, as ever. But he must definitely leave tomorrow. He'd planned to miss the scheduled city tour and spend this last day by the pool. Who was he kidding? He couldn't spend even an hour, let alone a whole day, in that dreadful place. He sat at the bar, becoming obsessed with the idea that he would just go, clear off; then he noticed that, while pondering the notion of 'clearing off', he'd emptied his glass. He asked the barman for another: 'Parakalo! Ena viski!'

Taking a sip of his drink seemed to calm him. At first, he didn't notice that his irrational anger and desire to leave had subsided. As if nothing had happened, he thought about the island ferries he'd seen the previous morning when he got up early to go down to the poolside. They were brilliant white in the sunshine. Like the seagulls that flew off from Piraeus to land on the sea. But those ships were going nowhere. They remained motionless, gleaming in the morning sunshine. There were dark stains on their rounded

23 The Turkish equivalent of f— off (with the dash) is used in the original text.

white bellies. The smoke from their funnels spread like fine down across the cloudless blue sky. When he left this hotel room and the loneliness of the rumpled bed, to return to the town where he lived, the ships would remain there, like toys; at sea without ever reaching a port. Because they were part of the scene. They made the mornings beautiful; the light was for them. They made the sea look blue, created the excitement of a voyage. He thought of last summer on the island of Hydra. Ships had gone back and forth, disgorging rowdy, almost rude, crowds of tourists, with nothing more to worry about than taking photographs, into the shabby streets of the island. The ships could be seen from the rooms overlooking the port. They went round the breakwater just beneath the end of the balcony and set off into the distance. That summer, everything had been in a state of flux. Even the words of the tanned blonde he was with had taken wing in that hushed room; they had flown out through the window and been scattered over the sea.

'Here are the special houses of Hydra, agapimu. See how big and beautiful they are, like castles!'

The stone houses facing the secluded harbour were built into the rocky hillside of the island. They were four- or five-storeyed, with iron bars on the windows. Their courtyards were surrounded by high walls. The facades, more like ramparts than walls, threw shadows on the blue and white awnings of the cafés and restaurants around the harbour; the shadows brought to mind medieval castles, concealing their narrow doorways for defensive purposes. It was a bit eerie, actually. Who knows? Maybe there were corroded bombs, arrow slits or dark corridors, all invisible from the outside? Provisions heaped in the cellars. Wheat, salted meats and huge earthenware jars of olive oil, enough to last for months, in case of a siege…

'These houses belong to people born and bred on Hydra. Look, that's Admiral Koundouriotis's house. And that one over there is the house of Berik Tombazis. We're standing on the island of the trading bourgeoisie who established the Greek state. The island of the people who fought against you!'

In the evening sun, the houses had appeared larger and more magnificent than they really were. His Greek lover had talked constantly ever since they rose from their midday sleep and began sipping whiskies on the sea-facing hotel balcony. She had spoken first about her country's history and then its relationships, the relationship between their countries; and from there, she had inevitably moved onto their own relationship. The vacuous words had glided from her mouth and up the masts of yachts chained up in the harbour. Even if he'd wanted to, he would have been unable to catch most of them. Then suddenly everything had become crystal clear: the sea, the summer sun, and what his lover was trying to say to him.

'That's how it is, Turkakimu.[24] We've fought and loved each other for centuries. Our love is as old as these houses. In fact, it's even older. When your Fatih took the Peloponnese, the people there took shelter on these islands. The people who came to Hydra built the houses you see here - later, they took up piracy.' He'd told her that he didn't know much about houses.

Now, here he was in the bar at Astir Palace in Vuliagmeni, alone with his memories of a summer that was as remote as Hydra's mountain monasteries. And for some reason he found himself thinking of a white-painted house with a blue door.

'Clearly these houses don't interest you. Actually, I don't much like houses that look like castles. Our house should be small. A white-painted house with a blue door, opening onto a garden of pomegranate trees. We should be able to draw water from the well. To water the flowers in the evening. Our daughters should have your eyes and my intellect.'

24. My little Turk (affectionate).

To grow old in a house, sharing a pillow, getting married and having children. Putting down roots like a pomegranate tree in a garden. To regret, at the moment of death, not really having lived your own life. Paralysed and a long way from what you have yearned for... With a strong feeling of suffocation, he'd decided to give up everything and leave, but then changed his mind.

Their relationship never recovered after his silence about those houses, or rather after her monologue. Yet everything had been so wonderful when they arrived on the island. So carefree, so transparent. They'd had no plans for the future. A hotel room overlooking the sea. Below, a small restaurant where they ate their meals. And the summer sun. That same old sun that was still burning his skin in the Astir Palace pool. Now, thank goodness, there was no woman with him, talking about the importance of houses. He was drinking alone at the bar. Tomorrow, he would pack up and go. Definitely. Yes, tomorrow he must stop prevaricating and clear off. Astir Palace seemed to symbolise the temporary nature of his existence in this world. This world? Or his adventures in this country?

'Astir Palace!' he repeated to himself. 'Sounds like Hastir pilaf...' and he roared with laughter. Then, suddenly becoming serious again, he said, 'Ena viski parakolo!'

The barman thought hard about how he was going to get rid of this foreigner who kept ordering more whiskies at such a late hour. In a decisive voice, he said in English 'We're closing now, sir.' The customer pretended not to hear.

'Ena viski parakolo!'

The barman switched off the cassette player and turned on the radio. Heavy, sorrowful night music filled the empty saloon. Then he placed a glass of whisky, with the bill, in front of the customer, saying, 'To logariyasmo, endaksi...'[25]

The night music on the radio stopped abruptly and the news came on. The customer listened intently to the female

25. The bill, right...

speaker who, barely pausing for breath, bombarded her listeners with a succession of bullet points.

Rising from their midday sleep, all those years ago, their bodies had been energetic, their minds alert. Shadows of the houses were falling over the sea. The woman beside him was talking incessantly, explaining something to him. Outside, the sun was setting. Ships were in the harbour.

The voice stopped abruptly when the barman switched the radio off. He pictured the ships out at sea setting sail. He signalled to the barman to turn the radio back on.

'We're closing now, sir. You'd better go up to your room now.'

He rose from his stool, lost his balance for a moment and looked as though he was about to fall. He pulled himself together immediately, and said, 'Kalinikhta' to the barman.

The barman, in a kinder and friendlier voice than on the previous night, said, 'Kalinikhta kiryos!'[26]

---

26. Goodnight, sir.

# The Woman on the Beach

SHE HAD GONE down to the beach as soon as she awoke from her midday sleep. Depressed and weary as always. Perhaps even more so than usual. The telephone had interrupted her sleep three times. Unable to get back to sleep after the third time, she'd gone out onto the hotel balcony and watched the comings and goings of the people down below. Blue, green and red parasols whose shade afforded no coolness, naked bodies burning on the sand and the August sun, still high in the sky. For a very brief instant, the sun had seemed to explode inside her head like a camera flash, making everything appear white. Naked bodies had begun to writhe in agony like jellyfish stranded on land.

Now she is on the beach under a sun that is no longer scorching hot, watching children playing at the seashore, pondering how colours suddenly melt and disappear, how a day leaves behind not even a handful of ash. Not even a handful of ash…

An old man selling sweetcorn drives a path through the crowd with the smoke from his trolley: 'Boiled sweetcorn!'

A simit-seller[27] beats his drum, shouting, 'Crisp and fresh!'

'Keep the kids happy!' yells a candyfloss seller. 'Mothers, candyfloss for your crying kids!' Whereupon sellers of candyfloss, grilled tripe, ice cream and nuts suddenly appear. Behind them come photographers, followed by a lemonade-seller, and a woman peddling clothes. The sound of the vendors is drowned by the voice of Zeki Müren[28] over a

---

27. Simit: a freshly baked sesame-covered pretzel.
28. Popular Turkish singer, similar in style and attire to Liberace.

loudspeaker:

'*Don't go, I need you always!*'

Is that what she should have said to him on the phone? She had said nothing. She didn't say, 'Again?' Nor did she say, 'Bon voyage!' Or, 'I'll miss you.' Her reply had been silence, a gradually intensifying silence.

'I'll call you from Paris.'

'...'

'Okay, in that case, I won't call. I'll never call ever again!'

'...'

'Do you think I'm happy about it? Do you think I like leaving you on your own like this? A beautiful young woman like you...'

'...'

'Say something, won't you? Swear and shout if you want. Just let me hear your voice.'

'...'

He'd slammed the phone down at her silence. He shouldn't have given her such confidence. And she had been very sure of herself. Whenever he said, 'A beautiful young woman like you,' he was always smiling beneath his moustache. It was true; she was beautiful. 'Different bed, different beauty in the mirror.' That's what he'd said when they first met. He always spoke through lines of poetry. 'Suddenly, acquaintance turned to love,' or, depending on the context, 'First kiss me, then bring me to life.' She may still have been beautiful, but she could no longer be considered young. She was a middle-aged woman in her prime, who had never had children. A single woman who was still fresh, still with an appetite for love-making, and who took pleasure in pleasing a man. Alone and anxious. The telephone rang again as she was taking a shower.

'I don't want to separate like this. Call in at Paris on your way to London!'

'Call in at Paris.' How many times had she heard those

words? 'Call in at Paris!' 'Come to Frankfurt!' 'Let's meet in Rome!' 'Fine, I'll come to London! But not straight away.' 'Is it my fault that the Channel's between us?' 'I can't come before Christmas!' 'The beginning of October's no good because of the university exams.' 'In April, I have a book coming out, and I've been asked to go to Spain in May. I can't go anywhere in May, but we could go away together in July, if you like. August? August is still a long way off. We'll think about it when summer comes…'

She could have said, 'I'm in the shower. Call me a bit later.'

She had let the cool water flow over her body. The drops had run from her curly blonde hair, spread down her neck, which was beginning to show signs of wrinkles, to her nipples, from where they had rolled down to her belly and disappeared. Her stomach muscles were still strong. For years, she had wanted a child from this man, who wandered from one city to another, one woman to another. She'd never had this desire with anyone else. He was the only one. His warmth, his sweet severity, the way he said, 'Oh, my one and only,' when reaching a climax - even if it was a lie. 'My one and only, my darling!' They were the best words she could hope to hear from this womaniser. Later, when their relationship had settled down, she had realised that she could never capture him, he would never be totally hers, and that she wanted a child from this man who kept slipping through her fingers. A little girl who looked like him. She was still under the shower when the telephone rang for the third time. She hadn't answered; if she had, she would have shouted out, 'Don't go!'

Now, as she sunbathes on the beach, she wants to shout out with Zeki Müren, 'Don't go! I need you always!', drowning the voices of the vendors, to call out as if in a trance, to the sea, wind and waves, and to the purple mountains in the distance, to rid her heart of pent-up bitterness, expectations and yearnings, of the ordeal - ordeals

- of their three years together; or rather their three years of separations. She wants to cry out: 'Don't go! I need you always!'

However, the song was soon over. And another one started. A cheerful, affected male voice started up with, *'Babe, where in Istanbul are you from?'* Well, I left Istanbul long ago. I'm from Maçka, or rather I was from Maçka. Because I live in England now. I live alone in London. Mayfair – where else? Lovers? Of course I have lovers! Fred, Jonathan, Alfred. And the one before Fred. And if you count those in Istanbul, Ali, Veli with the punk hair-do and earrings. And that bastard – who could forget that bastard! He was supposed to be calling from Paris...! She suddenly wanted to embrace him. To press her body against his and, just as he was about to enter her, to hold him by the hair and hurt him, to bite him all over. To bite a piece off him. He wouldn't have cared anyway. At that point, he would have felt nothing even if his fingernails were being pulled out.

The vendors reappeared when the hotel loudspeaker started playing 'Everywhere's in Darkness'. They had retreated to the far end of the beach and were now coming back. This time, they were joined by lottery ticket sellers. Their voices were suddenly drowned out by a record of Sezen Aksu. As they moved on, the 'disco' boat came into view. A bikini-clad woman was belly-dancing on the captain's bridge. She was accompanied by a hand-drum and a reed instrument played by Gypsies in white shirts that billowed in the wind like two sails. As the boat passed the end of the jetty, the 'Silver Cup Oriental Dance Show' at the Golf Disco was announced over the loudspeaker. It had barely passed when the Pilsen Disco boat appeared. There was a Beauty Queen Competition at the Pilsen Disco, as well as a raffle. Something for everyone. 'Everyone has a chance! Try your luck!' Yes, something for everyone! She smiled, thinking how coming across that man had been the real lottery prize. Where had that bookworm come from? He had affected her in a way that she had only ever heard or read about previously. She had felt compelled to meet this strange nomadic writer whose books tried to get at the inner feelings of women. One winter night, she had gone to Paris and knocked on his door. Door to what? It was more like a cave. He was living in a small, narrow attic room. It seemed as if he rarely went out and spent his life among books and the rustle of scattered papers. 'Who, if I cried out, would hear me among the angels' hierarchies?'[29] Yes, that's what he'd said, adding that Angel was the name of his wife, who had just left him.

Was she the only person to hear the cry of this lonely man, despairing in the hierarchies of angels on that bleak snowy night? It turned out that he was trying to recite one of Rilke's elegies because of a story he was writing. She had pressed the man's head to her bosom like a wounded bird and, with loving tenderness, wiped away the tears that were soaking his beard. 'My baby,' she had said. 'My big baby! I had to come and hear your voice!' They had rolled onto the floor together; without waiting to undress, in semi-nakedness, they had made love on the carpet. Semi-naked until morning, without separating or breaking away, without any separation, 'Wait, wait. Please, hold on!' she had cried, not out of fear of becoming pregnant, but to convince herself that he would not leave her again.

Actually, when she had cried out those first words of love 'Wait, wait. Please, hold on!' it was the first time she had been dishonest, which was something she had forgotten, or tried to forget while they were together. That moment suddenly surfaces and echoes in her consciousness. She returns to her room from the beach of this holiday town and the August heat where arabesque melodies blend with the voices of pedlars, and she lies naked on the white sheets. However much she cries out, 'Come! Please, don't hold on. Give me a baby!' her voice will not reach Paris, let alone

29. Duino Elegies - The First Elegy by Rainer Maria Rilke, translated by Stephen Mitchell.

the realm of angels. Their roles changed long ago; yes, she understands this now. She feels herself drawn back into the interrupted midday sleep. It is the first time she goes into decline.

I've had second thoughts about describing her second and third declines for the time being. We still have good days ahead of us. Passionate, jealous, twilight days. And our noisy love-making. At the moment, her hand is not in mine, nor is her slender blonde body beside me. Her tanned skin is not touching my skin. I feel sad that I left her alone on the beach like that. It would be untrue if I said I felt no fear on the plane when the 'Fasten your seatbelt' sign lit up for the third time. But the journey ends safely and we survive intact. Nevertheless, I'm very afraid of losing her while our relationship is having this little 'breathing space'. She's on the beach now. She's sleeping and she's forgotten all about the sun, the sea, us being side by side, the beds we have slept in. There are beads of perspiration on her brow, her hair is tousled. The boats anchored out at sea bob up and down in her large-framed sunglasses. I think about her eyelashes. How they fringe her eyelids. Long and still. But the world stirs in the sunglasses that cover those eyelashes. Children with bottles of water in their hands, young mothers busy with nature. Towels, swimsuits and sunhats move back and forth on the beach. It is clear from the twist of her lips that she has sunk into a deep sleep. When she is like that, the world becomes ugly. The sky, the mountains and the once deep blue sea gradually cloud and imperceptibly melt away to nothing. On the beach, the semi-naked bodies in their coloured swimsuits become a disgusting concoction in the heat. She is alone in this world, this pile of vomit of which I am a part. When she sleeps, she becomes pure and beautiful. Her thighs suddenly expand, her legs open. And her womanhood, which her swimsuit cannot conceal, becomes one with nature. She gives birth to our child while kissing the skies.

# The Award

*Yesterday, I looked down on you, dear Istanbul –*
Yahya Kemal Beyatli

AS THE MIST DISPERSES, he steeps himself in the city. The grey domes, the minarets, the slender Maiden's Tower. The opposite shore is not yet visible. Üsküdar is in a vague empty space. So is the Maiden's Tower; in the distance, you can just about see it rising out of the sea in the mist. Its red light flashes on and off. As the mist disperses, buildings, trees, roads appear. The first buses of the morning, first commuters, first steam of a ferry. He knows the drone will start with the new day. That untamed, unfamiliar, maddening and continuous drone of the city. Like a river slapping against leaking dykes. Or an ancient bus climbing a slope in second gear.

This noise had not stopped for years. It did not abate, even when the city silhouette had begun to fade from his memory, when the perpendiculars and curves had begun to overlap and merge discordantly, or when the blue of the sea, the green of the plane trees and the white of the city walls and stone buildings had dissolved into a dark colourlessness, a murky cloudiness, like the water of the Golden Horn. In the early hours of the morning, as the sun rose over the roofs of Paris, he always heard the sounds of his childhood. The crystal clear voice of the water-seller, the aged voice of the rag-and-bone man. It was not the monotonous sound of the Glacière metro that interrupted his sleep, but the rasping hoot of the ferries crossing the Bosphorus.

*Yesterday, I looked down on you, dear Istanbul.* He has finally returned. Like the last Ottoman poet, he is looking down on Istanbul. From the balcony of a room in the city's

115

tallest hotel. The mist is gradually dispersing. The September sun is shining down on the sea. On the shimmering ripples of the sea, on the seagulls, on the white of the ships anchored in the port. There are the royal gardens of Topkapi Palace, the Kubbealti,[30] the ugly park in Sarayburnu, the magnificent dome of Ayasofya. And the sharply pointed minarets of the Sultanahmet mosque. Over there, just beyond Süleymaniye, the entrance to the Golden Horn. The pigeons of Yeni Cami,[31] the crowds on Galata Bridge. And the city he has been away from for a lifetime, an endless separation.

*Endless separation,* he muses. It's a cliché, but how meaningful. Especially as you get older. However, the stories he writes aren't derived from phrases like these, or from the lyrics of arabesque melodies. He isn't yet completely attuned to social sensitivities. He doesn't, like many writers of his generation, make up stories from song titles such as *Endless Separation* or *Day Turns to Evening on the Quay of Yearning.* Yet it's true that separations don't end, and yearning doesn't diminish. *The Pain of Separation. If My Life is Over. The Past Tears my Heart Apart.* They're all wonderful! Especially the last one. So many stories and books have been named after it. It's true that the past tears at people's hearts and reduces them to ashes. *Ready to die for ideals or love.* Sometimes, scraps of lyrics like these come to his mind. *For years, while living far away / Wearied by dreams of Istanbul / My bursting brain could take no more.* He finds himself using silly words picked up here and there instead of writing symmetric, balanced phrases and serving up detailed love scenes in the style that excites his readers, especially female readers, and which critics have grown to accept and young intellectuals increasingly to adopt.

Undoubtedly, this prize was not given to him for his random use of such expressions. It was awarded for the first work of a writer in exile: *for expressing, in an original and*

30. In Topkapi Palace, where the Grand Vizier met with the Council of State.
31. New Mosque

*innovative style, the tragedy of a generation, the turmoil created among intellectuals by the military regime, the fatal harm inflicted by an era of oppression.*

The previous day, when they came to collect him from the airport, the director of the institution presenting the award held a press conference at which he said that the young generation should definitely read this book as a lesson about past experiments. He had responded by saying that he was happy to be back in Istanbul after so many years, but had then had suddenly come out with, 'Eeeeeendless separation. Eeeeeendless separation / The yearning in my heart never dieeeees / The paiiiiin, the paiiiiin of yearning.' They ignored his erroneous and inappropriate rendering of this song, and took it out of the TV news broadcast. After all, he was an internationally recognised writer who had just won the country's most prestigious literary award. Yet he obviously just wanted to joke about his homesickness and the pain of his lost years. They cut the press conference short, worried that he might start quoting the song 'If Only They'd Give Me Back Those Lost Years', bundled him into a car, brought him straight to this hotel - with the best view in the city - and left him here.

No-one, no-one at all, asked him out for dinner. The cocktail party in his honour was cancelled and the reprinting of his books halted. Now, as the mist disperses in the morning sun and the first light of day touches his sleep-deprived face, he looks at the city from the hotel balcony. He sees himself holding his mother's hand as he boards the Üsküdar ferry. How serious he is in his short trousers, polished shoes and black jacket. They're going to visit his father's grave. Later, his mother will leave him in the cool of the poplars rustling in the breeze while she reads the Fatiha. A voice, distant but also very close, will whisper words that he will hear for years to come. The first words of a story that he is to start in a café in the Place de Sorbonne but somehow will be unable to finish:

*My dear Dad, that simple man,*
*Has left me, gone away.*

He sees himself reading a book in the shade of a plane
tree in the rear garden of Galatasaray Lycée. It will soon be
evening. Now, in the dormitory, in the dim light of the blue
lamp, he will be able to continue his secret journey, guided
by words. He sees himself going down the street of brothels
in Kuledibi, as if going down to a well. His spotty face, his
cloudy eyes. A schoolbag in his hand, his palms sticky with
sweat. Those same hands are holding the hand of a blue-eyed
girl in a café in Beyazit. That evening, in a velvet armchair
in an attic room, the same evening that the police raid the
University of Technology hostel and kill Vedat Demircioglu
– *They shot and killed Vedat Demirciogu!* – he has his first taste
of passion. His first taste of the pleasure of love-making with
a woman without paying. And his first pain, first separation,
and first encounter with death in Taksim Square.

The march had started in front of the university. The
demonstration proceeded from Beyazit Square to Çagaloglu
and from there to Eminönü, growing all the time, like an
avalanche rolling down a slope, spilling over the police
barricade at the entrance to the bridge and down towards
Dolmabahçe. He remembers how they sang songs of
independence in front of ships of the American Sixth Fleet
that were anchored in the Bosphorus. *They were only kids,*
*surely you could see / They just wanted freedom, they were shouting*
*to be free!* Then the procession climbed up towards Taksim
Square. He was right at the front. The blue-eyed girl was
by his side. They were hand in hand. As they entered the
square, the police split up the procession by encircling the
first thousand or so protestors and taking them to the Taksim
Promenade where they were left as fodder for the attacks
of reactionaries who were armed with sticks and stones.
He remembers how, in the panic, he lost sight of his first
girlfriend and how, seeing his friends being knifed under the
gaze of the police, he ran for his life into the basement of an

apartment block. Yes, one morning years later, on a balcony of the Etap Marmara Hotel, he remembers that Bloody Sunday.[32] From where he is, Taksim Square is not visible.

But he does not think about the things that are visible, only what is not visible - or rather what was witnessed and forgotten. He has kept those images of Istanbul alive in his memory for years. The friends who died untimely deaths and those they left behind. Now, as he looks at the city stirring below, the crowded sunny streets leading down to the sea and the dark facades of the humming buildings, things he hasn't seen for years and will never see again surface in his consciousness. He pictures the demolished century-old buildings of Tarlabasi, the ramshackle houses by the shores of the Golden Horn, the narrow streets, the flame-haired girls on the four beautiful ceramics representing the four seasons, at the Markiz Cake Shop. It was noon in the August heat and he was sitting with friends, tragically now dead, drinking small carafes of raki in the bar beneath the bridge opposite some old ships rusting away in the Golden Horn, when a skiff appeared out of the blue and approached the jetty at the Persembe Bazaar. The boatman jumped ashore in a state of panic.

'Watch out! Watch out!' he shouted. 'Watch out for the fire! Fire! Watch out for the fire!'

The police carted the poor man off, either to the police station or the lunatic asylum, where his feet would be whipped until he was subdued. But he was right. What fires! What destruction! That bar beneath the bridge no longer exists. Nor the Persembe Bazaar. He read in the papers how they poured concrete onto the shores, how so many places were destroyed and beautiful buildings razed to the ground, how green squares with ancient Byzantine cisterns were turned into rubbish dumps, how a causeway was constructed in front of old the villas at Arnavutköy, which were not

32. Refers to the event in 1969 called Kanli Pazar, when police handed out sticks to rightists to attack leftists during a demonstration in Istanbul.

visible from where he was. He learned all this without setting foot in Istanbul. Everything that happened, and everything that was still going on! It was a cry from the heart that he tried to express at the press conference. The ashes of a fire, the dust of a destruction unseen until then. *The ashes of a fire –* a song best sung by Zeki Müren – yes, the ashes of a fire…

Random lyrics start going round in his head again. In order to escape, just for a moment, the accusatory images and nightmares of the past, and to focus on being back in Istanbul, he tries to remember the previous night. Because that was the true prize this city had given him.

It was nearly midnight when the telephone rang.

'Sir, you have a visitor.'

'At this time of night?'

'It's a lady. She insists on seeing you.'

'Very well. Show her up.'

He understood from the knock at the door. It was so apprehensive, so nervous. There she was with her blue eyes; she appeared out of the Istanbul night and was standing in front of him. Beneath her low-cut outfit, she was almost naked. Her small mouth, short-cropped blond hair and moist lips – just as when they first met. Years had not passed, time had stood still. They were hand in hand. Separation had not intervened, death had not taken its toll.

'I heard it on the television. Congratulations.'

'…'

'Absolutely the right decision. It was the best book. What a pity you don't write like that these days.'

Back then, he had kissed her trembling lips, then her hair. This time, years later, he hugged and embraced that award earned through the might of his pen, without letting go until morning.

Now alone, without optimism, he looks down on dear Istanbul. And he sees none of the places he had frequented and loved.

# Place de la Sorbonne

I'VE REACHED THE age at which my father died. In the words of Cahit Sitki, 'halfway there'[33]. It's not really halfway; I've lived an extra year in what Dante refers to as 'the dark woods'. Is that because I've strayed from the right road? Midway upon the road of our life I found / myself within a dark / wood, for the right way had been missed…'[34] I'm not going to discuss the concept of the word 'right' here. I just want to say that my father, with his deep blue eyes peering through round-framed spectacles, his fair curly hair and pale face, the father who now lives in photographs, will always be the age at which he died. He will remain the age at which he died, whereas I…

I'm sitting in the Café Ecritoire in the Place de la Sorbonne. In French, the name of the café means 'writing desk'. I know nothing about such desks, but the world of writing, of blank paper and words, this strange world that I would define as a form of existence, has become something I have been unable to give up or live without since my childhood. Yet I've written little. And everything I've written I have either not published or been unable to publish because of censorship. I've spent many days without writing anything. But for me, writing is an existential activity. And today in the Café Ecritoire, because I can't help myself, I write: 'People may be able to escape a neurosis, but never

33. Reference to 'Yas 35 Yolun Yarisi Eder' [Aged 35, Halfway There] by Cahit Sitki.
34. Dante, *The Divine Comedy*, I-ii, 'The Inferno', trans Charles Eliot Norton.

themselves.'

I'm sitting at a table next to the window. In front of me is the Place de la Sorbonne. A white-painted building, one of Paris's oddities, rises above a friend's newly opened reprographics workshop called 'Papyros'. Its six floors and attic have not been repaired for a long time. The first time I saw this square, that same building was standing there opposite the café, but the trees had not yet shed their leaves. Now, about twenty years later, I'm at the Ecritoire again. Writing desks existed before paper. People used to write on papyrus. And before that, on clay tablets. Nowadays, some writers use computers, but I prefer to stick with the blank paper I know so well. If writing means getting things wrong, erasing words and replacing them with others to construct a sentence, why is it out of step with the times to insist on using paper? To get *Crime and Punishment* to the printers on time, Dostoyevsky used to dictate to a young secretary - Anna Grigoriyevna - whom he later married. It's well known that the master drafted his novels in his head beforehand, right down to the last detail, so that when it came to the business of writing, he simply transferred them onto paper with hardly any changes. Yet I generally have no idea to which abyss the words following the first sentence will lead me. This work was planned as an experiment in autobiography, but I certainly don't know where it will take me, down which dead ends or around which twists and turns it will lead me. I'd read about Dostoyevsky dictating *Crime and Punishment* to Anna Grigoriyevna in my mother's translation of Henri Troyat's biography, *Dostoyevsky*.[35] But this recollection is definitely not going to get me very far now, in the Place de la Sorbonne. My mother spent one year at the Hôtel de Suez on the Boulevard Saint-Michel, a little further on from here. That was in 1962, the year my father was killed in a bus crash. No matter what time does to memories, the locations don't change. The same sun that lit up the windows of the

35. Published in English as *Firebrand: The Life of Dostoevsky* (Heinemann, 1946).

Hôtel de Suez, when my mother was there, is now shining on the Sorbonne church, cleansing the walls of hundreds of years of grime. On its dome is a cross, and above is a bright blue sky. Just below the dome is a clock, which has stopped at half-past eleven, for some reason. Exactly half past eleven. But time goes on. How many times have I been to this café? How many times has the setting sun shone on it? Just as the trees continue to grow and shed their leaves.

I'm looking at the statues on either side of the clock. How remote from the present day they seem with their long skirts and lifeless eyes. As if they exist in another time, in an unidentified dream. The other statues, which face the square on each side of the church, are the same. I know that the sun will now be shining on the cobbled courtyard of the Sorbonne. Students will be engrossed in conversation on the steps leading up to the library. The corridors, the lecture halls, and the cramped rooms overlooking the inner courtyard at the back are dark. How many times have I passed down those corridors? How many times have I lost my way in the labyrinth of knowledge before climbing to the archive section above the library? But I've never been crushed by the weight of what is to be found in books. If I ever find the 'right road', if one day the dark woods are illuminated, that miracle will be down to art, not science.

If I get up now and go up the steps of the Sorbonne, as I did in my student days, I'll pass the statue of Hugo looking pensively at the cobbled courtyard. As Nazim Hikmet said: 'Neither smiles nor streets are what make a city great / But the monuments to its poets.'[36] Which means Paris is a great city. How many times have I passed in front of this statue? Just as I've passed monuments to Mayakovsky in Moscow, Pushkin in Leningrad, and Bruno in the Campo dei Fiori in Rome. It would always be with the same feeling of enthusiasm, such as after Professor Etiemble's seminars or when I raised my head from the loneliness of lamp-lit sheets

36. Nazim Hikmet; *Sofya'dan* [From Sofya].

of blank paper or ancient tomes of knowledge, that I would pass this statue as I went out into the courtyard - perhaps to have a cigarette. It was the same when I passed in front of the statues of Ronsard, Montaigne and Balzac. It's true; Paris is a great city. But my lifespan is short. It's strange that a mere thirty years ago Paris was just a word for me. It had no real significance; it was just a word I tried to decipher from the scribbled handwriting on the back of postcard from my distant father: 'I'm in Paris,' my father used to write. 'This is the view from my hotel room.' Of course, I had no idea that the 'view' from a window of the Hôtel Select in 1958 was a view of the Place de la Sorbonne.

Similarly, I was not to know that one night, years later, a story, which I'd started but was unable to finish, the story of a contemporary Telemachus who set out to find his father in Paris, would direct me to the Hôtel Select. That night, instead of returning home, I had come to this hotel seeking traces of my father, who had stayed in a room on the third floor, and who had lived in photographs for so long; the light-complexioned curly-haired man I had such vague memories of. I will never know how he lived or what he did while he was staying at this hotel in 1958. But the curiosity aroused in me by the coloured postcards he sent to Balikesir is still there. I had recently learned to read. I was the 'pride and joy' of September 6th Primary School,[37] Miss Iffet's favourite pupil. I was only able to decipher the name of the city where my father stayed; the handwriting on the back of the card meant nothing to me without my mother's help. The Place de la Sorbonne had not yet entered my life. 'This is the view from my hotel room.'

My father spent one year at the Hôtel Select. As for me, my whole youth was spent in hotels. Later when I set off on my travels like a rudderless ship, I was forever waking up in hotel rooms. But I didn't always wake up alone. At

37. September 6th 1922 is celebrated as the day that the town of Balikesir was liberated from Greek occupation.

my side were beautiful flame-haired women, and in front of me views I never tired of. In my anthology *Sevgilim Istanbul*, in those stories set in Athens, Avignon, Paris, Marrakesh, Algiers, Constantine, Moscow, Leningrad and New York, I wrote of sinking into bed with a woman in hotel rooms and of the pleasure of waking tired after a night of lovemaking. Also of the pain of separation.

I am at the Café Ecritoire in the Place de la Sorbonne. How could I have known in 1958, when this square first entered my consciousness, when I was beginning to read, that for me this place would later have such a hold on me, that it would one day be part of the rhythm of my daily life? For ten years I've been coming here at least once a week. And before that I spent almost every day here while studying for my MA and PhD. I used to frequent the rows of bookshops on either side of the square, and I'd meet up with friends and lovers from all over the world at the Café Ecritoire.

I recall a photograph. It was taken one evening when we came to the Ecritoire after one of Etiemble's seminars. Six people around a table. We're happy. Still young, very young. Long years still stretch ahead of us. Professor Etiemble, who warned us against any kind of dogma and succeeded in opening our minds to different cultures, had not yet retired and withdrawn into obscurity. And Catherine! That tragedy of a girl who spoke seven languages. That dear friend who lay down on her bed one evening in Paris, turned on the gas and never rose again. And Yannick, that beautiful chocolate-coloured girl. She became my lover later. Maybe she is on a beach under the scorching sun in her own country now. Maybe she has incurred the wrath of the government and died under torture. I haven't heard from her since she left her doctorate half-finished and returned to Haiti.

There are others in the photo too. Fred, Alexander, Ali, Monika… I know their faces, but nothing about their destinies. This was student life at the Sorbonne… Paris, not

France, seemed like the whole world then. I think I should write a story based on this photograph, about embarking on life, about our lost beliefs, broken taboos, loves and friendships, and separations. Especially separations. Once again, a line of Nazim Hikmet comes to mind: 'Like seed, I have scattered my dead all over the world.'[38] Anyone who has passed through the Sorbonne could utter this line at some point in their lives. I am saying it at the halfway stage of my life. At the age my father died. I don't feel 'indescribable sorrow'[39] but I find I'm gradually missing more and more the things and people I love. Especially if they are far away, especially if there is no hope of meeting again, especially if they have dropped out of my life completely, especially... Who said 'the taste of yearning is not what it used to be?' The taste of yearning is stronger than it ever was before.

38. Nazim Hikmet; 'Dörtlük'. The poem refers to his second wife (who died in Odessa), Orhan Veli (who died in Istanbul) and another close friend, Nevsal (who died in Prague).
39. Orhan Veli; 'Istanbul Türküsü'.

# A Face in the Mountains

## Sunset

AN IMPECCABLE CLEAR sky. Brilliant deep blue. Redness had spread behind rocks scorched in the day by fierce mountain sunshine and eroded at night by snowstorms and cold winds. The colour of the sky gradually dimmed and lights went on in the distance. The sun would no longer illuminate the whiteness of the snow-covered slopes, or the rooftops and stained-glass windows of the church in the small town that stood where the valley opened out. It would not be reflected in the windows. It would no longer shine on the silent streets or the frozen water of the pool in the town square. Below, in the inhabited world, dusk fell and lights came on. Pools and rivers darkened. Above, a few stars appeared over the peaks beyond the precipitous cliffs and deep gorges. The sky slowly faded and the blue deepened. The sound of the pine forest ceased. It was barely audible anyway, inaudible to the returning skiers in their coloured sweaters and woollen hats.

A frightening silence descended over the few houses scattered around the mountainside. People retreated inside from their wooden balconies. A crowd from a cable car dispersed into hotel corridors, and darkness filled the sudden emptiness, like a rolling avalanche. The whiteness of the snow lit up the evening. The rocky mountain slopes and the snow-covered valley below were barely visible.

Just then, a gunshot was heard from the forest. The sound did not echo up in the mountains or down in the gorges. The pine trees trembled for a moment, but no more. A few birds flew out of the branches. Then everything was buried in a soft velvety silence. Night had fallen. The sound of the bullet was not heard by the smiling well-dressed people, with healthy faces tanned by mountain sunshine and athletic bodies relaxed after hot showers, who were making their way down carpeted stairways to magnificent hotel lounges. If they had, it would not have occurred to them that a pistol fired into the sunset would disturb the snowy slopes and the transparency of a gradually fading sky, or that, far away, an antique mirror in a silent room overlooking an inner courtyard in a noisy town would shatter, as if hit by a bullet.

# The Mirror

I saw her for the first time at dawn. I was struck as if by lightning. Nobody had ever looked at me like that. I was squeezed between antique armchairs, Chinese vases and ivory boxes in a shop window, with a silver candlestick on either side of me. The crystal ashtray in front of me had not been moved for months. With every day that passed, I was becoming more stifled by the heavy, soporific atmosphere of the shop. The incongruity of the objects in the shop window made me feel uneasy and the movement of the crowds hurrying past intensified my loneliness. Despite my being in one of the city's busiest streets, nobody was interested in me. Of course, sometimes a dolled-up woman or well-dressed dude stopped in front of me, but they moved away as soon as they had checked their hair or straightened their clothes. All day long, streams of people, seas of blue, green and red cars, packed buses, coats, jackets, mackintoshes and umbrellas passed by. At first, I was perplexed by these images of a complex world and by the strange outfits of the people. Then, I grew used to the unstarched shirts, the bare-headed women, and the motorised vehicles. I too wanted to join in the street action that started in the early morning, to move with the buzz of the city. I was tired of the stifling air in the shop window, the crowd of objects that surrounded me, the ugly faces and pungent smell of the elderly customers who entered the shop.

The activity in the street slowed down towards evening. People returning from work with tired faces, jaded looks, and messy hair passed in front of me. The wall of the building across the road darkened as the street became deserted, and a greyish light shone on the iron-barred windows. The only thing looking at me was that dark wall. The haste of the colourful world outside and the indifference of the crowds intensified my loneliness; I felt sadness at being just a forgotten mirror in a shop window. At least I was a mirror with some class, a mirror that had seen something of life. Many a princess, fashionable celebrity and famous artist had looked at me. Of course, that was long ago, very long ago. In the days when I adorned a magnificent and beautiful salon. All the guests, the ladies and gentlemen who lived in the house - and even the servants - would focus their interest on me; I was never alone. I was happy there, on the white wall opposite the fireplace. But after I was sold, along with the other items in the drawing room, all I ever saw, once the indifferent crowd that poured past this antique shop window petered out, was a dark sooty wall - not counting the so-called best days of my life I spent in that garret. At night, before submitting myself, along with a number of unappealing objects (mostly new enough to be my grandchildren) to deep forgetfulness and the void of darkness, I was left alone with my memories. As the light faded, I was erased from the face of the earth. My earthly existence was suddenly annihilated; it was only in my memories that I lived and felt that I existed. I remembered the faces that had looked at me, their smiles, the ladies' evening gowns, the way they secretly poked out their tongues and winked, and so many other crazy, foolish things; then the tired, sorrowful looks and dark blue-green eyes. Unfortunately, I forgot most of those images while I was in that damned garret. My memory became dim in the darkness; shapes and colours became obliterated. This would last until dawn when the street activity would start all over again in the early hours of the morning. In the daylight, any memories would fade away, and the dreadful loneliness would commence. That was before I came across her.

I saw her first in the morning light. It was as if I had been struck by lightning. Nobody had ever looked at me that way. She detached herself from the crowd and stopped in front of me. Suddenly we were eye to eye. Immediately, I felt our destinies were linked and we would never part. Two enormous black eyes with long, long eyelashes looked at me. I felt an unfamiliar strength and a beautiful sense of deep understanding. It was as if I were not merely something superficial, not merely a gilded mirror, but as if I had set down roots in the heart of the shop window and was gradually becoming integrated into the world. The black twinkle in her eyes penetrated my surface to the very depths of my existence. I felt in me the paleness of her long slender face and the softness of her thick, black hair. Her large red mouth came close and remained in front of me for a while. We looked at each other. Days, months and years passed. Time had somehow stopped. They were eyes that would excite even a mirror which, like me, was a rational mirror of good pedigree that had seen better days. The commotion in the street, the morning crowd, had melted away. The buses and cars, the hats, and the sooty wall opposite, all gradually faded. I was filled with her eyes, with her freshly-washed, well-slept pale face, her thick, sensuous, slightly sulky lips. In my world, there was no room for anything else. Her hair and her eyes brought me to life. I existed only to feel her sparkling eyes boring into me. That is how it happened. One morning she entered my life with the morning light; she united with me and made me hers. I became her.

We went through a door and down a long dark corridor. She did not switch on the light. Then we entered a fairly large, airy room. I saw a bookcase, a telephone on a low sideboard, a divan and armchairs, and a picture on the wall. Pushing the door with her foot, she squeezed me into a smaller room and propped me up in front of a window overlooking a courtyard. I remained there for a while. Below, I could see a cobbled courtyard, the dirty bricks of the wall opposite, a shuttered window, and roofs gleaming in the sunshine. Later, she came back with a friend; together they moved me from where she had placed me and hung me, slightly tilted, in the middle of her bedroom wall. From there, I could see a large, high bed, a blue-shaded lamp, and a flower-covered wall opposite. The narrow room suddenly opened up. Its walls retreated and the pile of books heaped haphazardly on shelves at either side of the bed seemed less cramped; the light coming in through the window was brighter and more intense. After fixing me to the wall, they went into the next room where they sat talking. I remained alone for a while. At first, I found my surroundings strange; I could not get used to my new place. After all, I had been in the antique shop window to be looked at, to draw the attention of reluctant customers to the confusion of images passing outside. I had been for sale. Like the other objects in the window, I was there to be liked, to arouse interest, to be evaluated. So for me, this silent room, with its bed, books and window overlooking an inner courtyard, seemed a backward step from the shop window.

I found myself in a position that was somewhere between the garret where I had been shut away and my happy days in the salon. She had bought me, and then forgotten about me; even worse, the notion that she was no longer interested in me overwhelmed me with despair. I was now no different from other objects in the bedroom, like the blue-shaded lamp or the alarm clock. There was nothing special about me except for my usefulness. I realised that the depth of feeling I had sensed in her when she first looked at me in the shop window was gradually fading, and I was shrinking, inwards, towards my centrum, to where the hook that held me aloft screwed into my back.

My morning cheerfulness had suddenly evaporated and I was sinking into depression, when she stood there before me again. Her sparkling black eyes were burning. Then, for the first time, I saw her in full length. Her long hair hung down over shoulders. She was wearing a white figure-hugging sweater and red earrings. Below her velvet trousers were high-heeled black shoes, which shone alluringly. I had never seen such a well-proportioned, attractive body before. Once again, I was touched to the core; I felt my centrum expanding and pressing into the wall. She was standing right in front of me. The way she looked at me, her upright statuesque stance was getting to me. She was actually with me, face to face with me; we had melted into one another and become one. She flicked her hair back with her hand, pushed her breasts out a little and tilted her lovely head with the red earrings to one side. Putting her hands on her hips, she winked. Then she came right up to me and, with a single unexpected movement, suddenly removed her sweater. I saw her breasts brimming out of her bra. With another rapid movement, she peeled off her trousers. In her high-heeled shoes, she stood motionless like the marble statue that had been placed next to me in the antique shop window for a while. Bending her left knee, she looked at her shoe for a while, inspecting its shiny black leather and stiletto heel. For a moment, she turned those deep, penetrating eyes towards the floor and I felt a strange, almost painful, resentment. Then we were face to face again. Without looking away from me, she took off her bra. She left it on the floor with her sweater and trousers. Her slender manicured fingers traced over her nipples and neck. Then she removed her black lace panties and, holding them to her nose for a moment, inhaled deeply. The panties looked tiny in her hand. They were screwed up into a ball. She placed the panties carefully on the bed. For the first time, she stood before me completely naked, with her long legs, slender waist and large breasts. I was seeing a naked person for the first time. The morning sun had risen high above the roofs and was illuminating the room. But it was as if the light was coming from the naked body in front of me, rather than from outside. Her sparkling black eyes were a source of light. I almost died of happiness at seeing the radiance of her face, her beautiful neck and shapely legs. She remained like that for a long time. Motionless, naked like a marble statue, radiant as the sun. Then, she lay down on the bed and spread her legs, showing me a tiny down-covered mound with a dark pink, purple-lipped hollow, a deep well that descended into her body. When she was standing in front of me just before, I had seen a strange feathery place at the top of the triangle made by her legs, but had paid little attention to it. I had been entranced by her eyes, the proportions of her large breasts and slender waist, her rounded knee-caps - by everything about her. But as she lay on her back and opened her legs, her body changed. A strange hollow appeared which I had not seen until that day. Where her thighs met her groin, there was an aperture covered by long down which exposed a small, trembling opening that was difficult to make out. Sliding her right hand down from her nipples towards her belly, she began to trace over the place where the opening started and to part the dark pinkish-purple lips. The aperture expanded and suddenly a mountain flower, a pink-leaved black water lily opened up before me. At that moment, I felt an overwhelming inadequacy. She was looking at me from where she was lying, but not in the same way as when we had first come face to face. Her eyes had become strange; that penetrating look that had touched me so deeply was replaced by a blank, unfocused stare which gazed above and beyond me to a vacuum of nothingness. For a moment, I thought that I had lost her and her whole body had slipped away from me. Then, she began to move

133

with a regular motion. Her breathing became heavy and her hand motions became more rapid. She gave out small cries as her fingers went in and out of the hollow that had opened and expanded before me. A deep trembling spread through her body. As the movement of her right hand accelerated, she shouted and jerked her head from side to side. I could see beads of sweat on her temples and beneath her armpits. The movement was now very rapid and her thighs rose ten inches above the mattress. Her face and lips slackened. She groaned hoarsely from deep inside and, at that moment, I thought she had died. Her glazed eyes were staring vacantly. I was very frightened. I thought that I had lost her and that, even if she lay naked in front of me for ever, we would never come face to face again. Never again would her eyes penetrate to my core or be able to integrate with my centrum. I suddenly wanted to disappear. To be erased from the world, to dissolve in an eternity without light or imagery, to be shattered into pieces. Then she calmed down a bit and the movement of her fingers slowed down. I could feel her heart beating beneath her breasts, which were glistening with sweat. In the silence of the room, the books, blue lampshade and alarm clock by the bed were rocking. We caught each other's eye again. As we had a little while before. As we had the day we first met. We became one again, I became her.

That is how it was. I must say I would never have believed it if anyone had told me that a noble mirror, which had seen better days in one of the grand nineteenth century salons, and which years later was shut away in a garret and then sold to an antiques dealer, only to languish for months in a shop window, would fall madly in love with a young woman and be revived by her gaze, only come to life when she looked at it.

After this, I saw her slip into this reverie several times, her body trembling and shuddering. I listened to her rapid breaths, her small cries followed by hoarse groans, and her heartbeat. But she was not alone, as on the first day. She writhed about with various men, either standing up or on the bed. With the touch of her fingers and her large red mouth, she hardened them, and took them inside her, into the dark pink, purple-lipped opening in the downy aperture between her legs. Some men lay on top of her; others turned their backs to me and supported themselves with their hands against the wall. Sometimes, she looked at me as if she were alone on the bed, as if there was no-one else in the room, as if we had been together for years, while a man thrust himself back and forth on top of her body. That was when I loved her most. But her face was never as taut as on that first day; her eyes never again penetrated or moved me as much.

Some nights, when she slept alone, she would suddenly get up, switch on the lamp and lean towards me in the blue light. From her eyes, I would understand the horror of the dream she was having. She usually came home tired. All day long, I would wait for her opposite the floral-patterned wall and large unmade bed, in the loneliness of the grey light that filtered through the window. She would spend a while in the next room. I would think of her - stretched out on the divan I had seen on the day she brought me home - looking at the picture on the wall. In the picture was an impeccable, clear sky. Brilliant deep blue. Redness had spread behind rocks scorched in the day by fierce mountain sunshine and eroded at night by snowstorms and cold winds. A few stars had appeared above the peaks beyond the precipitous rocks and deep gorges. Lights were on in the distance. It was a picture of a mountain scene at the time when distant lights were turned on and the water began to darken. I would feel an unbearable desire for her to come and undress before me straight away. Sometimes she was late. She would fall asleep on the divan and come to me in the morning, tired and sallow-faced. Sometimes, she would lie on the bed in front of me reading a book which would slowly slip from her hands. Her eyelids would grow heavy and she would fall into a deep sleep without getting into bed. In the blue lamplight, I would observe her tired face, her dreams reflecting the book she had been reading, the moistness of her large mouth. That was how our days together passed.

One morning, I noticed a change in her appearance. It is difficult to explain, but her eyes had lost their sparkle and depth. There was a strange frozen look about them that I could not fathom. A distant look of yearning had appeared in her eyes. She still looked at me with love and sincerity. But it was as if it was not her looking at me. They were not the same dark eyes that had moved me and caused me to exist. She had hidden herself away and was looking out from there. But her hiding place kept changing. She did not see me. Or rather, she saw me, but took me for a stranger, or some unfamiliar object. I was no longer her; I could not integrate with her beautiful well-proportioned body, her long slender face and her lovely generous mouth; I could not be her. She was slipping away from me. It was as if she was not there. She still wanted to stand before me, leaning towards me and probing my depths with those black eyes, but she did not get through to my centrum, she did not reach deep inside me. I was suffering; it was unbearable having her so close, yet so distant.

For a while after that morning, we continued to come face-to-face, but maintained a certain distance between us. Yet her interest in me did not wane. She still woke in the night and switched on the lamp. She would stand in front of me with tousled hair and tired eyelashes. Sometimes she cried, sometimes she sat in front of me for hours until morning arrived. But she never looked at me as she had done the first time we came face-to-face, or during those happy days we spent together. Not once did I feel that I had expanded or deepened, or that I had grown in stature. Nevertheless, our lives carried on. We became distant from each other, but were not total strangers.

Then one day, she disappeared. It was the first time we had been separated. I thought she would return within a few days. But days passed, and the days turned into weeks and months. She did not return. She had left me alone, with the books on the wall opposite the unmade bed, the rarely used alarm clock, and the blue-shaded lamp, which was left permanently switched on. I do not remember how many times the sun rose above the roofs, or the rain poured down into the silence of the courtyard. It was as if time had stopped. The emptiness in the room was worse than death. At night, the forgotten lamp, which illuminated the stains on the sheets, the dusty shelves, and the fading blue flowers on the opposite wall, prevented me from being erased from the world for a single night, from melting into the colourless, shapeless forgetfulness of darkness. Time expanded and my loneliness increased during those endless days and nights. My world was filled with her absence and the emptiness of not having her with me. I watched, as the colours of the stained sheets fluctuated in the daylight, as the lamplight illuminated the books she once held with slender fingers and read with sparkling eyes. Dawn would break and the sun would rise above the roofs. Then darkness would fall over the courtyard. Rain fell; clouds dispersed. As the clouds dispersed, the sun came out again. At night, the room was lit by the lamp and dust gathered on the shelves and books. Morning came without her and daylight shone on me without her. Night fell without her and it ended without her. I lived with her absence.

One day, a tired woman arrived; she stood in front of me and looked at me. Her hair was cropped short and, with her enormous sunglasses, she had a mysterious look about her. Her face was deathly white and her lips were cracked. When she removed her glasses and leaned towards me, I recognised her. I was bewildered and filled with a sudden excitement. But the person in front of me was not her. She was looking at me with different eyes. With the unseeing eyes of a dead woman who looked out from another, distant world. Her black eyes were no longer my black eyes. Her long thin face was not my face, her forehead was not my forehead, and her body did not match mine. I was not her. I watched her trace her hand over her chapped lips and the lines on her forehead. As if wanting to ascertain the reality of her face, she inspected her temples with her fingers. She was wearing a long skirt. It was too large for her body and hung shapelessly around her. Beneath the skirt, her torn stockings were dirty. She removed her thick-heeled, scuffed shoes and lay down on the bed, staring at the ceiling. She remained there for a long time without stirring. Then she went to the next room and returned with a plastic bag in her hand. She emptied the contents of the bag onto the bed. Red, blue and yellow boxes of pills disappeared among the rumpled sheets. She arranged the boxes according to colour and size, examined each one carefully and lined them up on the dusty shelves. Some of them she hid carefully among some books. She lay down on the bed again and remained there, motionless. Towards evening she sat up and took a few pills from the box she had placed by her bed, and then let herself sink back into the inertia of the stained sheets.

At night, she lay in bed fully-clothed, half-asleep in the blue lamplight, making sounds that were sometimes strange wheezing noises, sometimes sounds of pain. As she lay there, I realised that her body was elsewhere, distancing herself from the world around her. For days, she did not leave her room. When she looked at me, it was not with her own eyes.

'They killed that girl,' she said to me one day. For a long time she caressed her semi-naked body with her hands. 'They killed a little girl,' she repeated, 'They put me in a glass jar. They surrounded me with glass walls. I see everything. You, the books, people walking in the streets. But I can't touch any of them. I'm alone inside the glass jar. Do you hear me? I'm alone inside a glass jar. Yes, alone, I said. Do you hear me? They'll arrive soon. They'll chew up my body and grind me to pieces. I hate them.'

She talked ceaselessly, then suddenly stopped, After a long silence, she pointed at me. 'You're my enemy,' she said. 'You killed her. Yes, you killed her.'

Outside there are people, buses, noisy cafés. The city's like an ants' nest,' she continued. 'Everybody is rushing about. But me – I'm alone in a glass jar.' Her eyes widened. 'Horrible animals will eat that little girl!' she shouted. 'Yes, they'll eat her. They'll tear her apart with their sharp teeth. The sun is entering my body,' she said. 'Light frightens me. I don't like the sun or light. Everything fills me up inside, yet I feel nothing of the world.'

Sometimes, she would reach out to touch the walls of the room with her hands, or she would lean against the window and press her lips to the glass. It was as if she wanted to be certain of these things, of the reality of the world around her. She stood in front of me, feeling her breasts and legs, looking at her body, that body previously touched by love, as if it was something alien. Her fingers inspected it, like a strange set of objects, as she tried to find and understand herself.

'You,' she said to me. 'You came to me to kill her mother. You tore her baby to pieces. That beautiful silver-haired baby. The mother's dead anyway. She's dead and turned to dust. She didn't love her, and then she died. Teach me how to hate without loving. Little girls like me pour into the world all the time. Always crying, they keep coming. Then walls are built and they're shut away in a room. They're shut away and they cry.'

Then she started to cry. 'I was fine in the clinic,' she gulped, without wiping her eyes. 'I was really fine. There were clean white sheets on the beds and linden trees in the garden. I was fine under the trees, but I don't want to go back there. The world is empty; my body, my inside is empty. I'm in a wasteland. Do you hear me?' she said. 'I can't bear the electric shocks; they're going to kill me. They're going to kill me!'

139

Sometimes, she came up to me and talked nonsensically about all sorts of things. One day she was going to die; another day she was going to kill me. She said she was frightened of everyone, very frightened. I've forgotten most of what she said.

One night, she came home with a man who was strange, like she was. I remember that they shouted at each other like animals; they were afraid of each other and bit each other all over as they made love. Before the man left, he left her a jet black, toy-like pistol. She went to bed clutching the pistol. In the morning, she stood before me stark naked. Her hair had grown, and there were fewer lines on her forehead. A little colour had come into her lips and her eyes looked more alive. Like the day I first saw her naked. She pointed the pistol towards me and made as if to fire it. I was not afraid. I felt death inside me, penetrating deep into my centrum. Then she dressed, left the room, and never came back.

# A Face in the Mountains

An impeccable, clear sky. Brilliant deep blue. Redness has spread behind rocks scorched in the day by fierce mountain sunshine and eroded at night by snowstorms and cold winds. The colour of the sky gradually dims and lights are on in the distance.

She is lying in the forest. Stretched out under a pine tree, her head and hands are bare. One arm wrapped around a tree trunk, the other arm buried in the earth. As if wanting to touch the soil and feel the roots of the tree. Her face is turned towards the sky; a gun lies next to her locks of hair. Blood is seeping from her temple; her eyes are motionless in the fading light. They stare vacantly, with a petrified look; blood has congealed on her eyelashes. Her sunglasses have slipped down towards her mouth, but do not completely cover her lips. The whiteness of the peaks beyond the precipitous cliffs and deep gorges is reflected in the lenses of her sunglasses. The world in the lenses is empty. So is the sky. The sunglasses reflect a sky-blue wasteland. All images of her train journey to the hotel at the foot of this mountain, where she came to breathe the mountain air that was so essential to her, have been wiped clean. No longer are fields, houses and towns flashing past the convex glass. There are no images of trees, widening and narrowing roads or crowded stations reflected in the lenses of her sunglasses. Now, in the depths of this silent forest, she clutches at the trunk of a tree, as if trying to capture the mercurial, inviolable quality of the natural world, a world that has slipped from her consciousness. That same natural world she saw from the train window, that was reflected in her glasses, yet did not reach her. Her slender fingers on the gnarled unforgiving trunk. Above her, the tree is darkening, its thick branches untouched by the yellow light from the mountains. It is as if she wants to feel not only the tree's existence, but that of the whole forest. Her fingers are clutching so hard, her arms wrapped around it so tightly. She wants to feel the tangible reality of the rapidly changing scenes that flashed past the train as it sped through the countryside without stopping at any stations, the natural world that was reflected as a confusion of colours and shapes in her sunglasses, to feel the existence of unfathomable villages, with their bridges, rivers and cart tracks - in short, she wants to feel the world of human beings. It is not just with her arms, but with her entire body, her entire existence that she hugs the tree. She wants to prove that she has lived, that she was real; she wants to merge with the world.

Soon snow will cover her face. Night will fill her eyes. Her entire body will disappear in a snowstorm. Her hair and nails will cease to grow anymore. The red mountain sun will be unable to warm her beneath the snow. But, with the arrival of spring, the snow will melt into water that will flow from the damp trunk of this gnarled tree and into her frozen body, untouched by earth or decay, and the sap of the tree will rise in her still extant form. The body that was lost to the antique mirror in her silent room overlooking an inner courtyard in a distant noisy city will be filled with the world. The sap will rise in the ends of her frozen fingers and her blood-soaked hair. Her eyes and breasts will come to life. Her black eyes will regain their sparkle. Her large red mouth will become moist. The sun will warm her bare legs beneath her coat. The downy, deep pink, purple-lipped creature beneath her belly will awaken from its winter sleep. It will rise and yawn with desire. Then, in the mountains, the face will be taut with pleasure. It will groan with a husky voice from deep, deep inside. At that moment, the mirror of the clear impeccable sky will expand and deepen. But now, opposite a wall, on which hangs a picture of a sunset in the mountains, on a low sideboard next to an empty divan, the telephone keeps ringing.

# Before the Summer Comes

I HAD NOT expected summer to appear so early that year. After all, we had experienced a long, hard winter. Grey mornings, rainy evenings that plunged the city into darkness without waiting for the neon street lamps to come on, mists that descended over the parks and the Seine - these were still fresh in the memory. We were living through the timid, uncertain days of spring. The sun was out one minute, hidden the next, creating sudden and unexpected darkness. Our room would fill with claps of thunder that reached right into the most secluded corners and alleyways of the city. Houses, smoky basement cafes, and even the tunnels of the Métro echoed with thunder. Above, clouds would gather over roofs, belfries and balconies, and spring rain would fall, at first warm and mild, then gradually turning into a cold, merciless downpour, later to be replaced by a fine drizzle that lasted until morning. Even if we thought the next day would start with brilliant sunshine, bathed and cleansed by night frost and dense, misty darkness, we would suspect that the familiar wind would rise as evening fell. That wind, which smelled of seaweed, and which travelled right through Paris, beneath its bridges, in and out of the open-topped chests of riverside booksellers, would bring more rain. The sun would illuminate people walking to work in the mornings, the boulevard cafes, the globular wine glasses that we called 'balloons', and then retreat, and clouds would cast shadows along the city streets. And suddenly, another clap of thunder, followed by warm spring rain that chilled as night fell.

While living through such uncertain, changeable days,

it was only natural that I did not expect to be faced with summer so suddenly. Summer had been a probability for us, a probability that we had kept postponing, leaving it to the familiar flow of nature during the winter. But it was not really a probability; it was a certainty, a clear-cut decision. It was something we had expected and planned for. We knew, whatever else transpired, that it would come knocking at our door one day. It had to happen, because of the desire which we had exhausted, set aside, then completely forgotten about and lost during winter, and because of the hopeless familiarity that had alienated us both, first from ourselves, then from each other.

Anyway, I had prepared myself for this time; I was in tune with the seasons. Everything had to take its course and reach its natural end. A year ago, I had expected my loneliness, when I could no longer wake up with the warmth of a familiar body by my side, to coincide with summer. Summer would come in all its natural glory and embrace my existence at the allotted time. Say, for instance, at the quiet of midday when no shadows sprouted from cool roots of trees and spread into the streets from dark courtyards. Or at night, when, as I lay perspiring on the bed, my stiffening penis pressing down without hope onto stained sheets.

I could say I was going to greet summer like the cunning Mexican cowboy in the films of my childhood. Melancholy and motionless, like a Mexican dozing against a wall, his straw hat pulled down. Melancholy and motionless, but always on the alert. Like that agile Mexican, who cool-headedly awaits a bullet from an ambush; who, in the nick of time, can render useless the barrel of a gun directed at his forehead, or a poisonous arrow aimed at his heart by a Red Indian. However, it did not turn out as I had expected. Summer arrived suddenly, with the haste of a swallow. It was not a summer of lengthening days that warmed the earth and brought green to the trees. Nor of laughter from the Japanese tourists filling the hotels of Paris and taking photographs in front of Notre Dame Cathedral, the Panthéon and Sacré Coeur, nor of the silence of suddenly deserted tree-lined boulevards. These familiar images of summer were still a long way off. Warmth had not yet reached the flowers in the Luxembourg Gardens. Sweaters and umbrellas had not yet been stored away in box rooms. Nevertheless, summer had still arrived.

Summer was in the train ticket she took out of her handbag and placed on the table when she returned home in the evening. Separation suddenly revealed itself during momentary glimpses of sunshine in the uncertain days of spring, in the rain that started warm and turned to sleet. Despite knowing beforehand that it would happen, I had not expected summer to come early that year, or her sudden departure on a day in April, before the days had even started to lengthen or the earth to warm.

'Three months either way – what's the difference?' she said, putting the train ticket back in her handbag and sitting down next to me. 'Anyway, we both wanted this separation.'

It was true. We had both wanted to go our separate ways, and had even decided on the date and time. She would fly to Tunis on the morning of July 5th, and from there to the city of Sfaks. She had found a teaching post for the forthcoming academic year and even signed a two-year contract. This separation was no bolt from the blue that was suddenly wrecking our relationship. But, to be honest, I was not expecting her to leave me so suddenly, before we had even reached July. I had prepared myself for life without her during the days of summer. But now, while waiting for summer, I had to endure the tension of her unexpected departure before summer had even arrived. I was tired. Even though it was impossible for us to make love and touch each other with the same desire as before, it was comfortable to share a bed with her and feel the warmth of her body against my skin in the mornings. Moreover, I still loved her. I loved the generous way she still gave herself to me, and I loved to gaze at her body, which still aroused desire and excitement in me, but could not be sated. In fact, it was sufficient for me merely to think about that mysterious cleft, now a little less amenable than before, and the slippery softness within, which had once drawn my whole being to her. Her womanhood came alive in my imagination and I could create endless erotic images without needing to make love with her. After all, we had experimented together. We had felt the whip of lust together, and been tossed in the whirlwind of physical union.

'We both wanted this separation,' she repeated. 'Anyway, it's better like this.'

'How come?'

'I'll go to Rome and stay with my father for a while. I'll write to you from there.'

Her father was the French ambassador in Rome. He had wanted to leave Paris after her mother went to live with someone else; he was posted first to Madrid and then to Rome. Things were not too good between them.

'No, don't write anything to me,' I said. 'I want us to have a complete break. But not now. When summer comes. Let's end this in summer. As we decided – in July.'

She smiled. 'You're never going to change. And you shouldn't change. You must always be like this – intense, obsessed.'

We were supposed to go our separate ways one year after we met. In summer, in the heat of July. When even the tree roots had no shadows around them.

'I'd planned for your absence. I'd imagined my life without you at midday in July.' How could I describe to her the sick image of my desire to wander the streets of Paris under a ferocious summer sun? 'I'd planned for your absence,' I repeated. 'My life without you was meant to start at noon on a July day in one of the deserted boulevard cafés, when everyone's gone on holiday. I was going to sit there downing glasses of chilled muscadet from those clear round balloons.'

'And you would have been eyeing up some American chick sitting at the next table...' she said, not finishing her sentence. She was trying to make light of the situation.

'True. There would have to be a flirtatious American girl with long legs, wearing  enormous sunglasses and eating ice-cream!'

She had started writing a novel. A love story entitled *A Summer in Paris*. We could have discussed that phrase all night, until the morning of her departure. She would have proposed certain scenarios and we could have elaborated on the personalities, towns and relationships. We were living in a make-believe world. Perhaps our declining sexual desire for each other was a natural end to this gradually disintegrating existence. It was as if my imagination was struggling to achieve something that the closeness of our bodies had failed to do. I suddenly felt bored, and wanted to change the subject.

'American women don't come to Paris for their summer holidays any more. The only tourists are the Japanese who go round all the city's monuments, or any vertical bit of stone, with cameras in their hands.'

'Is that so?' she smiled. 'And you? You're a tourist, aren't you?'

She loosened the knot of hair at her neck and stretched out on the bed. I saw myself going up the escalator in the Odéon Métro towards ground level. Anaesthetised by alcohol, I had submitted my body to the motion of the escalator; my eyes were staring vacantly into space. Danton's statue was getting closer. He was so sure of himself; who knows what he was pointing at like that. His forefinger was directed straight ahead. Trees, more trees and a patch of sky... I was on another escalator at Alésia, having difficulty remaining upright. I had been wandering about all day, walking down streets, through parks and across squares.

Paris was quivering inside me. I was in its cafés and among the crowds in its streets. Almost everywhere I turned, a monument or statue appeared in front of me. I dived down some narrow, unknown streets for a while. When it started to rain, I took shelter in the Métro and travelled underground through the city. I was on an escalator again. Sounds were coming from the world below, which was hollowed out like a mole's nest. I would soon emerge at ground level into the illuminated boulevard. I would walk past the stone walls of Alésia Cathedral, and some cinemas. In order to shut myself away in my room, in my loneliness. To submit my tired body to the softness of night.

I saw myself in a taxi going down Boulevard Raspail. On either side were dark, silent buildings. It was like going down a tunnel. Lights had been switched off long ago. The boulevard was completely deserted in the rain. I was passing quickly under the trees, watching the traffic lights at the intersection turn green, briefly orange and then red – they stayed red for a long time. The colours were reflected on the tarmac of the wet boulevard. Soon, I would cross to the other side of the river. Then, then… I would head upwards from Boulevard Opéra and hurl myself into the arms of a woman with cut glass between her damp thighs and a huge cavernous mouth… I saw myself in a taxi going along rue de Saint Jacques. I was travelling quickly towards the city centre. I was returning to my room in the early hours of the morning. A dim light was shining on the walls. Advertising hoardings showed long-legged, naked women with painted lips. I was returning to my room, tired and sleepy, after a long night. To my coffin, from the body of the woman who awaited me every night in the area above Boulevard Opéra…

'You're a tourist too, aren't you?' she repeated.

'That was before I met you. Flitting from one street to another, one woman to another – that was what I did before I met you.'

She did not reply. She just looked into my eyes. We gazed at each other for a long time. After a while, she touched my temple with her hand and traced her slender fingers over my face. I took hold of her wrist and pulled her towards me. She did not resist. We sat opposite each other on the bed for a while. Then she wrapped her arms around my neck and hugged me tightly. I felt myself react to the warmth of her breasts. They were quite small, firm breasts. More alive than ever. I felt the beating of her heart, not in my heart but in my groin. We rolled over on the bed.

'Explore my body a little,' she murmured. 'You never know what unexpected alleyways you might find.'

Her breathing was becoming more rapid, yet I realised that the hand with which she was peeling off my trousers was performing a duty, as it had for years, a duty that was now routine. My desire, which had spread and intensified in my groin when she pressed her breasts to my body, slowly subsided. Which unexpected alleyways? What hidden charms to suddenly entice a stranger or curious tourist? I knew every bit of that body. All its nooks and crannies, its twists and turns, its hills and valleys, its bumps – everything. Even the ravines beyond the dead ends and the dizzying breezes of those sheer precipices were etched in my memory. After quickly peeling off her trousers and tossing them to the corner of the room, she wrapped her arms around my neck again. Then she relaxed her hold and gazed up at the ceiling. Her heart was no longer beating as rapidly as before. One by one, I reluctantly removed my clothes and lowered myself onto the familiar nakedness of the body beneath me. As I slowly parted her legs, she murmured almost inaudibly, 'We could leave it until tomorrow, if you like.' I stroked her pale skin.

'Aren't you going tomorrow?'

'I'm supposed to be, but...'

She could not finish. There was a hint of weary hope in her voice. Suddenly, she made a decision:

'I'm going. And I'm never coming back.'

# Istanbul, My Love

I got to know you gradually. It was like discovering the secrets of a strange woman's body. Yet you were always there. According to the words of the Delphic oracle, ever since the people of Megara came to your shores and settled on the peninsula opposite the shores of the unseeing people in Kadiköy - and even long before that, when people first built reed shelters to protect them from predators at the place where the Kagithane river runs into the Golden Horn - you were there.

Your name was Lycos. The water that surrounded you on three sides was clear and filled with gleaming fish. Trees sighed in your forests. Your name was Byzantium. With your Acropolis, your Agora, your baths and your bronze statues of the gods, you were a small city at the tip of a peninsula. Your big-bellied ships set sail from your secluded harbours to the uncharitable open seas. Your people were earnest and industrious. Your name was Neo Roma. You were a magnificent Roman city, with your gates, your porphyry monuments, your Çemberlitas[40] and your vast Hippodrome, whose bronze statues of horses with tossing manes now rear up at the crowds of tourists in Venice's San Marco Square. Ships brought marble and gold to your ports.

Istanbul, you were always there. You were there before time began. Your name was Constantinople. With your city ramparts that proved impregnable three times, your crenellated walls, your towers, flags and palaces, your stone

40. Burnt Column - erected 330 AD to celebrate the designation of Constantinople as capital of the Roman Empire.

houses overlooking the sea, with your preachers, churches, monasteries, sacred springs and icons, your monks and your angels – you were the capital city of a large empire. Your name was Constantinople where, visible even from Uludag, history's first dome rose to a starry sky, like an upturned abyss, on the top of Ayasofya. Mosaics, giant columns of green porphyry, golden crowns and silver candelabra gleamed in the light that poured in through the arched windows. Light illuminated galleries large enough to hold all your citizens; it lit up walls and even narrow corridors, the number of which was known only to monks. Then, as now, storks flew over you in the migration season. There were no pointed minarets piercing the sky, but the storks heading for Mecca, the orangey-purple clouds, the shearwaters and cormorants were all there then. And the shadow of Galata Tower fell on the roofs of houses and the narrow streets lined with Genoese cafés. You had no equal, with your shoals of fish teaming through the Bosphorus to the Marmara Sea, brought by the south-westerly *lodos* and north-easterly *poyraz* winds. You were always there, Istanbul!

Your name was Dar-i Saadet.[41] And the call to prayer was chanted in Ayasofya. Sultan Fatih, a rose in his hand, drove your ships over land. Pigeons drank from the water troughs at Eyüpsultan. Your name was Dar ül-Hilafe.[42] White stones were chiselled; lead, for bullets, was melted in enormous crucibles; porcelain, painted with tulips, pomegranate blossoms and green meadows, was baked in kilns. The depths, proportions and domed arches of the Süleymaniye Mosque were forming in the imagination of the architect Sinan. Crowds consisting of Albanians, Bosnians, Greeks, Jews, Armenians, Turks, Arabs, Circassians and Georgians, swelled by Genoese and Venetians, filled your vaulted bazaars. The unseeing found their way by the smell of spring flowers; ships loaded with wheat set sail for Venice, Genoa and Marseilles.

41. Gateway of Happiness
42. Gateway of the Caliphate

Your name was Dar-i Devlet-i Aliye-i Osmaniye.[43] The Grand Vizier, viziers, army pashas, the Sheikh ul-Islam and treasury officials appeared with their weighty turbans and swishing kaftans; janissaries mutinied and made demands. Princes suffocated in your prisons. Mothers and wives of sultans, favoured courtesans, concubines and dark-skinned eunuchs groomed themselves in the Harem. At the entrance to the palace, the Cellat Cesmesi[44] flowed continuously. The sea too flowed, in front of the Palace Peninsula. But you remained in place. When earthquakes occurred, houses, mosques, minarets, schools, and bridges collapsed; everything was razed to the ground. A mosque dome or palace ceiling would fall, exposing Byzantine mosaics to the daylight. Bubonic plague swept through your ports. By the Bosphorus, villas, mansions and timber houses blazed. But all were rebuilt. Those lost in earthquakes, fires and wars, and those who died of the plague, were replaced by the new-born. Years, centuries passed. You were at the point where three seas met. Your name was Lycos and Byzantium. Your name was Dar-i Saadet, Dar ül-Hilafe and Dar-i Devlet-i Aliye-i Osmaniye. And it was Istanbul. It was the City. Yes, the City.

How many years is it? How many years since I gazed at your sea, saw your people, walked in your streets and alleys, crossed your squares? Now, in Paris's rue du Figuier, far away from you, I am with you. A short while ago, I saw an advertisement. Boats setting sail with the angels of Ayasofya. They had grown wings and were flying with the dome, which is said to be held together by mortar mixed with the spittle of the Prophet Mohammed. Another advertisement showed sparkling water. You were gleaming in the sun with your blue sea, white ships, ferry boats, sailing dinghies and barges, your lobsters, crabs and a myriad of colourful fish.

43. Gateway of the Great Ottoman State
44. Executioner's Fountain

'AYASOFYA BOSPHORUS HOTEL' and 'FISH: 2000 Francs, SUN and SEA: FREE!' You are now a place that can be reached by anyone with two thousand francs and a little time to spare. But I cannot reach you. I cannot touch your sea or the dirty, cloudy water of the Golden Horn; I cannot caress your domes, your minarets or your towers. How many years is it...? How long since I sat in your waterside cafes, rubbed my face against your sooty walls, walked along your ramparts, climbed your peaks and fortifications? How many years since I relaxed in the shade of your plane trees? Now, here in Figuier Street, in a secluded room overlooking the courtyard of Hôtel de Sens, hunched over sheets of blank paper, I think of you. In the lamplight, you slowly take shape. Your domes and minarets. Your winding streets, your wide avenues. The entrance to the Bosphorus, the dirty waters of the Golden Horn. And the silence. The silence of your school courtyards, your cemeteries, your cisterns! The light! The dim grey light of overcast skies. The sun glinting on the windows of Üsküdar and the trembling flame of the candle in front of the icon of the Holy Mary. The blue light of the dormitory and my loneliness. Yes, my loneliness. My yearning for you even when in your midst. 'Two things are lost when we die: the memories of our mother's face and of our city.' So said a famous Istanbul poet[45] – a great poet who suffered much during his long separations from home. From a distance, I caress your round white face, your protruding cheekbones. As I touch your moist body, my fingers burn. You are rising from my ashes, Istanbul!

---

45. Nazim Hikmet

# The Assembly of Dead Souls

MARRAKESH, MY DARLING, is an oasis city in the south of Morocco, which fans out towards the foothills of the snow-capped Atlas Mountains. It was established as a resting place for the weary, lumbering camels and nomadic 'blue men' of the Western Sahara, whose caravans carried salt and gold from Africa to the Mediterranean. The Koutoubia minaret rises to the sky among the city's red-walled houses and palm trees, proving that Islam has been in Marrakesh since the twelfth century. The Koutoubia is an ancient and beautiful mosque built by the Almohads, who were Berbers from the south of the country. It used to be surrounded by bookshops, but now children play football on the vacant land. I've been spending my time in Marrakesh at the Jamaa el-Fna, or Assembly of Dead Souls, which is at the entrance to the old city and where the condemned were executed.

This place is an unbelievable celebration of tragedy; the pandemonium is such as I've never seen before in any other city or country, or even encountered in adventure stories. I say tragedy, because the blend of charm and destitution in the faces that fill the Assembly of Dead Souls reminds me of horror movies that combine bitter reality with surrealism.

Imagine a place controlled by a blind republic and a kingdom of beggars: snake swallowers and teeth extractors, impassioned Koran reciters and medicinal herb sellers, veiled women and young girls, water sellers, vagabonds, cripples, children – especially the dark ones – like dried olives. The crowd moves and stops; a sea of colour that gradually blends into the colour of the desert evening, and shouts like a chorus in some strange nightmare. When they speak, they swallow their vowels and exaggerate their 'h's. An ugly, mean-looking man races desert rats. Another plays a shepherd's pipe, making a snake rise up and dance. He wears a jet-black jalaba beneath his white-streaked beard. Someone who appears to be an imam is explaining the night of Mir'aj[46] and the crowd responds with 'Allahuekbar'.[47] I'm listening to how Mohammad went from Mecca to Jerusalem, where he mingled with the prophets. A tanned, blind minstrel carrying a violin sings sweetly about the bitter end of 'Leyla and Majnun'. And there are sellers of hot soup, offal, meatballs, oil and yoghurt... It is a market that sells everything imaginable, from daggers to bracelets, mint to buttons. And, in the dying light, fried fish and boiled sheep's heads.

When I boarded the plane, it was minus five degrees in Paris and plus thirty in Marrakesh. Earth-coloured wall hangings, faded by the sun, depict desert cats. On entering the old city, I saw children playing with rubbish bins; and in Medina's narrow streets, twisted like intestines, were tired-looking men, and women with hennaed hands. There was a strange sorrow in their eyes. Their streets belonged to a city that had seen better days. They walked strangely, with a heavy, lurching limp, as if they were not of this world. I looked through a half-open door into a courtyard: a pool, with blue ceramic tiles and a wall hanging depicting the Kaaba.[48] As I tried to absorb this unexpected secret world that had suddenly appeared before me, the door - with Holy Fatima's hand on it - was shut in my face. I was excluded. Muslim Marrakesh did not show me its true face or the inside of its houses. I walked past the two-storey balconied houses of the Jewish quarter and came out into the Assembly of Dead Souls again. This time I headed straight for the market.

46. When Mohammad ascended into heaven
47. 'God is Great.'
48. Cuboid building at the centre — geographically and spiritually - of Mecca.

As soon as I passed under the arches, I felt a lovely coolness on my face. I passed freshly-cleaned shops and old men selling cheap jewellery. Suddenly, I found myself among mirrors. My face was split into a thousand pieces. Where was I now? Where were my hands and eyes? What was I looking at? Was that my face in the mirrors of this cool market? My face splintered into a thousand pieces of changing colour and form? Or a frightful spectre of a rootless foreigner? The lines on my forehead had become deep ravines, my beard the colour of copper. My nose and mouth were displaced. Who had hit me? Why had I disintegrated in this way? When had these pieces of me become scattered like this?

In Paris, there's a photograph on the wall of my room in rue du Figuier. It was taken years ago on your island, on Ikaria, remember? We were sitting on a kilim[49] under an olive tree. You were smiling in your usual radiant way; I was a bit subdued. We were both young, with years ahead of us. We were looking longingly at something. If it was an olive, it would have dried out in the midday sun; puckered and bitter. The olive tree was very ancient, with roots going deep into the earth. Behind us was a small, white-walled church. Like a miniature, no bigger than a house. Next to it were some island goats. There was something else in the photograph, but I don't remember what it was now. Perhaps it was your delight at seeing the wine-coloured sea of Ikaria; perhaps it was the desire in our eyes. Our total involvement with each other. Of course, I could not have known that we would start to make love that day on Ikaria under the olive tree in the village of Chrysostomos or that my body would suddenly stiffen and defy gravity between your legs. Somehow, I found myself inside you. Everything revolved – the earth, the tree, your body, the earth. The sap of the tree was rising from its roots into your body. There on the kilim, we became one. We no longer heard the sound of crickets. Your tongue was in my mouth, your hands in my palms.

49. Ornately woven rug.

Our bodies were locked together. At that moment, I could never have imagined that my body, trembling with pleasure, would suddenly take off like a breeze rising in the midday heat to hum through the rocks, as if the kilim was not on the earth and we were not on the kilim, as if the narrow hollow between your legs, lubricated by sap, opened out into a fathomless space.

I remember having a similar feeling, a sudden impression of stiffening and taking flight, when I was living in the low-ceilinged attic of a dilapidated house at the bottom of a street of brothels in Constantine.[50] While wandering around the crowded market of the city, which was perched on the rocks like an eagle's nest, I lost my way and found myself in one of the narrow streets that opened onto the cliff next to the suspension bridge. The street descended steeply down to the rocky cliff where the Rhumel flowed, and was lined with yellow- and blue-painted houses; I walked to the very end house, anticipating the dark-skinned woman who would take me into one of the rooms overhanging the cliff. I was naked on the bed. Through the open window I could see a clear blue sky - spotless and brilliant. I remember how the woman had entered the room silently and, turning her back to the window, had jumped on top of me with the energy and alertness of a long-maned thoroughbred, foaming at the mouth and panting heavily. She placed herself on my rearing groin and pulled me, trembling with fear, into the deep space between her legs. I was outside time and completely alone, erect like a distant lighthouse.

That day, on the island of Ikaria, you pulled me into a space not visible in the photo, into your own tempestuous depths. Perhaps you too have a copy of that photo, next to the bed you no longer share with me. How strange it is that, years later, I could easily be that olive tree. Twisted and bitter under the midday sun. Bitter towards the earth that binds its roots. Unable to get up and leave. Its roots can only go downwards into the ground. Its leaves do not even rustle in the crazy wind. Its shade is sufficient only for ants. That day, I had no idea that I could be as tempestuous as the waves crashing on the half-submerged rocks in the seas around Ikaria. And today, here in Marrakesh, you look out at me from the mirrors with the same tempestuousness. But you are not here; you are nowhere to be found. I know I lost you long ago.

I walked through the market of mirrors. I walked alone. I passed jewellers' shops, pedlars, herbalists and tailors. And I found myself once more in the Assembly of Dead Souls. All roads in Marrakesh lead to this place. Just as in Istanbul, where I used to wander around and always ended up in Taksim Square. At weekends, I would walk from one end of Istiklal Caddesi to the other and back again. Then, once or twice round the monument in Taksim Square. Buses would come and go. The skirt of a high school girl would billow up in the wind. Before returning to school, I would wander behind Siraselviler and back to Taksim again. You were not there then. Istanbul's narrow muddy streets were there, so was the south-west facing sea. And so was an indefinable woman, who entered my dreams in the blue night-light of the dormitory.

I am sitting on the top floor terrace of a café. The air is gradually becoming cool. The sun is descending towards the snow-capped Atlas Mountains. Noises rise up from the crowds milling in the square below. Who knows what is being sold, what tricks they are up to! I can hear the sound of a violin being played by the blind minstrel. He sits at the foot of a wall and talks continuously. Completely alone. But after a while, people start to appear from the outer suburbs, from beyond the city walls, from the bus stations; they take their places in the square to listen to the blind minstrel tell a story in a language that I don't understand. The same thing happens every evening when I sit down to have my coffee. The minstrel sits cross-legged at the foot of the earth-coloured wall, begins to play his violin, and a crowd of fakirs gathers around him. Weary men, veiled women, children. Despite the constant hum in the square, they listen in silence. They take no interest in the trading, or in the motor vehicles trying to make their way through the crowd. They have had their allotted share in this world and the world no longer interests them. They listen to the blind minstrel. And the minstrel tells a story which, though I don't understand him, I already know.

*Qays and Leyla loved each other even when they were children. There could be no Qays without Leyla, no Leyla without Qays…*

He starts telling the same story today. His voice is so beautiful. As if burned in the sun and rinsed in the sand. As if, instead of from the foot of the wall opposite, his voice is coming from the desert, from a vast country beyond the Atlas Mountains, bringing with it the light of the stars and the sparkle of fiery sand.

*Leyla fell in love with Qays at first sight. And Qays with Leyla.*

That is how love is in the Middle East. Lovers fall in love with each other at first sight. But in order to love, they have to overcome obstacles. They don't make a phone call and go to the other side of the world. When they find the one they love, they don't get up and leave. They can't leave. Love in the Middle East is for ever. And star-crossed lovers become crazy. Hark, the blind minstrel begins his narration. Hear the warnings of separation:

*They loved each other, but it was a star-crossed love. They did not give Leyla to Qays. Qays became crazy and collapsed in the desert. His love became the stuff of legend and he became known as Majnun.*[51]

In the evening sun, I see a crowd of fakirs gather around the blind minstrel. The men stand upright in their shabby jabalas. The women look sad, the children are mere skin and

51. Majnun - meaning crazy

bone. A young girl wipes away her tears with her veil and, pulling a child onto her lap, hugs it tightly. The voice of the blind minstrel seems closer, as if coming from the depths of the Earth. The sound of the violin whines a monotonous melody. The table, the cup on the table, and the tea in the cup, quiver.

*Majnun remained in the desert, without Leyla. In the day, he spoke with gazelles, at night with the stars. If there had been no Leyla, would any of this have happened to Majnun? They married Leyla to someone else. And Majnun remained crazy, just as this sad story of love remains an echo of this false world.*

My love, evening is falling on the Assembly of Dead Souls. Shadows are lengthening in the twilight. Before long, lights will come on and the crowds will disperse.

*They take Majnun to Kaaba to recover. Majnun wants to die from his misfortune in love. 'Oh God! Kill me with this misfortune of love. Never release me from love's misfortune,' he says. He says nothing more.*

Yes, the crowds will soon disperse and lights will come on in the houses. Everyone will leave and I will be left alone in this café. The blind minstrel will also be left alone, but he will not finish his story. Why should he finish? Do I? Do I break my pen because I have no reader? The voice of the minstrel is very close to me now. I feel his words rising up from within me. He will say:

*When Leyla came to the desert to see Majnun, he did not recognise her. Who is Leyla? Who is Majnun? And what is love? What is passion? 'If the lover's content with mere dreams of her kiss, why then does she feign such reluctance?'*[52]

It was truly a star-crossed passion. Now, in a similar way, I travel the world without you. Without you, yet passionately in love. I go from one town to another, one woman to another. I frequently make love and take off. My body has lost its heaviness; it has risen in the vacuum. And travel has drawn me to its depths like a passionate sea. The

52. *Leyla and Majnun* – epic poem based on the Arabic legend, by Fuzuli, 1535

voice of the blind minstrel has stopped. He will have stuffed his violin under his arm and disappeared, feeling his way down the dark street. The Assembly of Dead Souls is now deserted. Evening has fallen in Marrakesh.

# The Return

THE ROAD LINED with poplar trees, the bridge, the narrow, steeply rising street. I watched the cat at the end of the street. It climbed up the crumbling garden wall, into the mulberry tree, and from there onto the roof, where it clung to the chimney. Dense grey smoke was dispersing in the wind. The cat went into the smoke, emerged and then disappeared between the tiles of the roof. I stopped in front of the garden gate.

If I entered now, the journey would be over. 'Life ends, but the journey goes on for ever.' It was written on walls in towns and hotels. On the white sides of ships, on the front of trains and aeroplanes. In waiting rooms, on station clocks, on the windscreens of trucks and buses. Or else some familiar voice would keep whispering those words in my ear: 'Life ends, but the journey goes on for ever.' If I entered, there would be no more knocks on the door of my room in rue du Figuier in Paris. Neither the telephone nor the bells of Notre Dame would ring again. At night, there would be no Turkish words congregating in the light of the lamp. The exile would be over. If I entered, I would find you on the divan in the living room. Your hair white, patience written on your pale, round face.

'So, you came back.'

'I came back.'

'While you were away, the trees were blighted by frost. They've all rotted away.'

'But I see nothing's happened to the mulberry tree.'

'It's like me – falling to bits.'

'No, no. You look great! You're looking very well.'

'I've grown old now. I tell you, I'm worn out. Don't do it again!'

'...'

'You went away. Don't do it again.'

'...'

'Haven't you had enough out of life? Aren't you satisfied yet with what you've had out of this world?'

'...'

You're right, it should be the last time. I won't leave again. I didn't know I would be away for so long and that you'd age so much. Everything's rotting away. When I was last here, frost was blighting the trees. The garden was covered with couch grass, the water level in the cistern was going down. But now, how strange… It's as if summer has not yet started. As if the rain has not fallen. The earth has dried out, and the withered leaves are trembling almost imperceptibly. Clearly, the wind isn't bringing any rain. Water isn't getting to the branches. How strange… It's as if the house is deserted. The covers haven't been taken off the armchairs, and there's a layer of dust on the divan. No hand has touched the Koran on the wall for a long time. Even the ever-faithful chiming clock has stopped. Dirty walls, rooms; steps to the garden, the silence of the wooden balcony… Everything, everything is stuck in the past. A distant loneliness has descended over your eyes. As if you're not there, as if you're not sitting there looking at me. You don't look at me with tenderness. When you turn away from the window to look at your son for the first time in years, your eyes are frozen and lifeless. If you would only smile a little, the whiteness of the walls would revive. The ticking of the clock would fill the living room. The dust on the divan and Koran would suddenly disappear; the water would reach up to the branches. But you do not smile.

'I waited so long for you. Endless days and nights.'

'Well, I'm here. I came back in the end.'

'Yes, you came back. But you aren't what I was waiting for.'

So, I'm not what you were waiting for. True, you were waiting for somebody else. You've been waiting for the infant you rocked on your knee in the shade of the mulberry tree in the garden, the child whom you tucked up at night and whose prayers you blew out into the darkness of the night, the smiling adolescent in the photograph on the wall of the guest room. Because, since the deaths of those close to you, especially your husband, you have been totally alone in this timber house. Your life was his life, your world consisted of his existence. The day began with him and ended with him at night. He was your reason for living. Naturally, you were expecting the adolescent – for whom you had once sprinkled water to wish him a safe journey to Paris – the adolescent who had wept and reeled at leaving his mother. You did not expect this weary, bearded man who suddenly appeared in front of you as if by the magic of Aladdin's lamp.

If only you knew what sorrow, what loneliness this man has suffered. How he has been tossed from one town to another, from one woman to another. His life has been spent in cramped rooms and dark streets. He's flown across oceans in aeroplanes more enormous than you could ever imagine even in your dreams, wandered through noisy city streets and parks. But he didn't forget your round, white face, or your warmth. He saw you in Paris, in the cloudy waters of the Seine beneath the Pont Marie, on the blank paper when the streetlamps came on in rue du Figuier. Your hands, your face and your broad forehead. When snow was falling in Moscow's Pushkin Square, you were on his mind. And when listening to jazz in one of those Greenwich Village dives. No sunshine, not even the scorching sun of the Mediterranean could ever warm his soul like you. Now, years later, you're right to say that this weary man you see in front of you today is not the person you were waiting for.

Yet he has kept waiting for this moment, this day of return. You must understand that.

'Don't you recognise your son? Were you waiting for someone other than me?'

'...'

'Well, I came back. This is the last time. If I leave again, the journey will never end.'

'...'

I stopped in front of the garden gate. If I entered now, the gate would close tightly behind me. The moment I went up the stairs to the living room, it would be the end of Paris. The brightly-lit, crowded boulevards, the cafes, the beautiful women, everything – it would all end. So what if it ended? It was time for me to live there in that timber house with you, time I adopted a sober way of life. We'd restore the house and sort out the garden. The earth would be revitalised, water would reach the branches again. You'd see the leaves of the mulberry tree, in whose shade I once slept, become green, thick and strong again.

I opened the gate and entered the garden. It wasn't as neglected as I had supposed. Everything was in place: the mulberry tree, the stone wall, the unused cistern in the corner. I inhaled the smell of earth and my excitement abated a little. The tension in my body relaxed. The time had come. Time for me to go up to the living room. How many years was it? How many years since I had seen you, heard your voice? How many years since I had heard your footsteps on the wooden floor of the living room? I used to feel the house shake. The walls, windowpanes would tremble, the darkness deepen. But that would all stop the moment you entered the room. The darkness would disappear; the world would light up in your face. I needed to tell you that the deepest, best sleep I ever experienced was not when you said a prayer and blew it out into the darkness, but on a summer day, cradled in your lap. In the cool shade of the mulberry tree, while the cistern rumbled. Now, it was the sounds of the cities I'd inhabited that rumbled inside me. I needed to tell you things that I'd wanted to say to you but until that day had been unable to: my first crime, first punishment, all the 'firsts' in my life. I needed to come to you and tell you about the cities I'd seen, the women I'd known, everything, everything in a single breath.

Without wasting time in the garden, I went up the steps and knocked on the door; there was a strange silence. I waited for a while. When nobody answered, I knocked again. Still no sound. Just then, I felt a soft-haired creature brush my ankles. Looking down, I saw it was a cat. It rushed down the steps and ran to the far end of the garden, jumped over the stone wall and disappeared. Seeing the cat reminded me that I'd seen smoke coming out of the chimney. This time I knocked as hard as I could. The door opened. An elderly, headscarved woman stood in front of me.

'Who were you looking for?'

'...'

'Are you by any chance Nurhayat Hanim's son?'

I rushed inside. Nobody was there.

'I'm Nurhayat Hanim's neighbour. Haci's wife. You obviously didn't get the telegram we sent to Paris. Your mother passed away...'

I collapsed onto the divan. Light was streaming into the room where you had waited for me all those years. But you were not there.

# Istanbul, Agapi Mu![53]

They were feeling tired in the dark little room. It was the end of a day of travel and pleasure. A dim light shone through the narrow gap in the curtains. It glittered on the woman's tanned skin for a moment, bleaching her body. The man mused that he would never be able to forget this naked Mediterranean body lying next to him, that he would always yearn for this body during the endless summer days on the beach, in the city's cool, breezy cafés, before and during sleep punctuated by his dreams and nightmares. He felt a strange loneliness. It was more than merely desire and sorrow; it was a beautiful loneliness that struck him deep inside and, instead of sweeping him away, enveloped him like a wave. The daylight moved from the woman's perspiring body to the man's face, and then to the wall where it lit up the dusty globe of the lamp. As soon as the curtain began to stir in the evening breeze, the light would be gone.

They were lying side-by-side in the dark, on the narrow bed. The man reached out to switch on the lamp, but then thought better of it. For a moment, his hand was suspended indecisively. He looked at his fingers. His fingernails were all in place. He thought of dead friends lying beneath the earth, whose fingernails no longer grew. He remembered those he had lost. Ageing, sorrowful faces; drooping, slackening skin. Departing women, separations, early deaths... Suddenly, sensing that the body beside him was coming to life, he grasped the woman's hips. He felt goose pimples break out on her skin beneath his fingertips. Before his hand entered

53. 'Istanbul, My Love' in phonetic Greek.

the slippery moist cleft, he heard her heavy breathing as she whispered those foreign words in his ear. Their bodies interlocked.

When they awoke, the room was dark. It was filled with the sounds of the city coming in through the open window. Horns, brakes, human voices, street vendors' cries, the flapping of pigeons' wings, and the hooting of ferries; an indistinguishable confusion of sounds embraced their beings like a distant moan.

The woman thought about their relationship. She wanted to relive her days in this unique city, poised between West and East, surrounded by sea, its people, shanty towns and narrow, undulating streets spreading out haphazardly in an unruly and defiant manner. She wanted to revive memories of the days she had spent with the man she had encountered in this Middle Eastern city, with its mix of old and new, past and present – this noisy city, the 'Constantinople' of her school books. But even though she had been dreaming of this journey for years, she could recall very little from those days, other than a few indistinct images. In her mind, she had assembled images of the Istanbul inhabited by her ancestors for over a thousand years, a combination of fact and fantasy, created from things she had heard and read.

She felt as if a cloud, which kept changing shape and colour, had penetrated deep into her mind, spreading a strange decomposing ache in her memory. The cloud had then been split open and swept away by perpendicular and circular lines. The city's silhouette was formed of long slender minarets, voluminous domes, towers, ramparts, turrets and a few skyscrapers. She remembered the dim grey walls, the pigeons and the coolness of the café by the mosque courtyard where they used to drink tea. Once again she saw the corpse of a cat floating in the Golden Horn, where scum gathered in the tarry, muddy waters. She screwed up her face in disgust. Then she relaxed, remembering the sea and the sunlight shining on the ships anchored in the distance.

Coolness spread through her body, as if the water of the Bosphorus that flowed from the Black Sea to the Marmara was coursing through her veins.

They were in a taxi. The deep, ultramarine water was flowing past them. As the road narrowed, the trees multiplied. Ships the size of cities passed rapidly by, with gulls hovering over their foamy wash. Caiques and cormorants bobbed up and down on the water as they cut through the brilliant white foam. Bay-windowed timber houses intermixed with concrete buildings. Occasionally, the dark windows of an old villa, their red ochre paint peeling, would flash past. Then, high garden walls, narrow streets leading down to the sea, and trees... trees... Steamships passed, their fishing nets drying in the sun. Small white steamships. At the most unexpected moments, when they reached a curve or turning in the road, graves appeared in front of them. Magnificent stone turbans with ancient words twisting and curling beneath. Then suddenly, they arrived at the quayside and were sitting under a noble plane tree, shaded by clouds that cast a coppery glow over the water.

Next, they were hand-in-hand on a street. The street went straight down a slope, leading them past houses of rotting, patched timber and empty plots of land. Elderly women in headscarves were stationed at the windows, peering through geraniums and sweet basil, watching out for cats. This street, which eventually led down to the sea somehow, brought them out into a vegetable garden. Not knowing what to do in their confusion at finding themselves among tomato stakes and giant green beans, they entwined themselves passionately around each other.

Next, they were in a noisy high street. They lost each other as they tried to make their way through the crowds spilling off the pavement. When they found each other again, they walked past some humming buildings of stone that looked ready to topple down on them, and then squeezed themselves into a churchyard where the street narrowed. In the silence of the churchyard, they listened to their hearts beating in time with each other, as if they were one. From the churchyard, they went down a moss-covered stone stairway to the cistern where they kissed at length in the coolness of the oozing, ancient Byzantine walls.

In the darkness of the room, the woman was absorbed with her impressions of the city. It was as if she had forgotten that it was with the man lying next to her that she'd discovered this city and the streets they'd wandered through, the shady plane trees they'd relaxed under after mingling in the crowds of the markets and streets, the steamships, taxis and noisy buses they'd boarded. The man with whom she had rushed from one shore to the other, from mosque to church, from one museum to the next, was lying right beside her and had just been inside her, striving to give her satisfaction. This city had drawn her femininity in among its meandering streets, aqueducts, underpasses and overpasses, its crumbling city walls. It had captured her, was taking advantage of her. Its towers and minarets seemed to be pressing against her skin, spreading a subtle ache throughout her body.

'I'm not really what you want,' he said.

The woman did not reply. She recalled the image of an ancient icon, its colours faded. It reminded her of the one that stood by the bed of her grandmother in Athens. Mary's long, narrow face was sorrowful. She was holding Jesus in her arms. The infant Jesus, who was neither of her own body nor of her own life. On the walls of Ayasofya, Byzantine angels were poised for flight. There was a blue gleam in their terrifying eyes. In a secluded monastery courtyard, an elderly priest was frying fish in a pan. He stared in amazement as the colourful, floured fish leapt into the pool at his side and disappeared into the water. The sound of canons was coming from the city walls.

'It wasn't me that you caressed and made love to all night,' he continued.

The woman said nothing. She had no wish to give

an answer to this tired, foreign man who did not speak her language. She thought of her life beyond the dark, curtained room, of the evening crowds congregating outside. The city, its alleys and backstreets, the continual rumble of vehicles on the roads, its walls, its houses, its rooms - rooms where naked couples made love - they all seemed to be flowing past like a light at sea. She knew she could never let herself be part of that flow.

'The ship leaves very early tomorrow. You must get ready,' he said.

Get ready. Pack everything into the suitcase. This untidy bed, the hotel room, the city outside. She realised that certain things which had been a part of her existence for years and had taken root in her subconscious, things which she had thought were her own, were gradually disengaging from her body and slipping away.

'Istanbul agapi mu!' she whispered to the man. They clasped each other tightly again.

# About the Author

**Nedim Gürsel** has been described by Yashar Kemal as 'one of the few contemporary Turkish writers who have brought something new to our literature.' Born in Gaziantep, Turkey, in 1951, Gürsel was forced – after the coup d'état in 1971 – to testify in court over one of his articles, which lead to his temporay exile in France, where he studied at the Sorbonne. Gürsel then returned to Turkey, but the military putsch of 1980 sent him back into exile in France. He was awarded the Prize of the Academy of Turkish Linguistics and Literature for his first major prose work, *A Long Summer in Istanbul* (1975), which has been translated into several languages. In 1986, his novel *La Première Femme* received the Ipeçki Prize for its contribution to conciliation between the Greek and Turkish peoples. His autobiography *Au Pays des Poissons Captifs* was recently published simultaneously in France and Turkey. He faced trial in 2009 for 'denigrating religious values' in his novel, *The Daughters of Allah*, which was also awarded the Freedom of Expression and Publishing Award. His first novel to be translated into English, *The Conqueror*, was published by Talisman, New York, in 2010.

# About the Translator

**Ruth Whitehouse** worked for thirty years as a professional violinist before taking a PhD in Modern Turkish Literature at SOAS. She's the translator of the novels *Ali and Ramazan* by Perihan Magden (Everest, 2011), and *Hotel Bosphorus* by Esmahan Akyol (Bitter Lemon Press, 2011), and the short stories 'The Well' by Türker Armaner, 'A Question' by Müge Iplikçi (both in *The Book of Istanbul*, Comma Press, 2010), and 'Fig Seed' by Feryal Tilmaç, broadcast on BBC Radio 4 in 2010. She is a member of the Cunda International Workshop for Translators of Turkish Literature.

# The Book of Istanbul

## A CITY IN SHORT FICTION
Ed. Jim Hinks & Gul Turner

978-1905583317

£7.99

Featuring:
Türker Armaner - Murat Gülsoy - Nedim Gürsel - Muge
Iplikci - Karin Karakasli - Sema Kaygusuz - Gönül Kivilcim
- Mario Levi - Özen Yula - Mehmet Zaman Saçlioglu

Istanbul. Seat of empire. Melting pot where East meets
West. Fingertip touching-point between two continents.

Even today there are many different versions of the city,
different communities, distinct peoples, each with their
own turbulent past and challenging interpretation of the
present; each providing a distinct topography on which the
fictions of the city can play out.

This book brings together ten short stories from some
of Turkey's leading writers, taking us on a literary tour
of the city, from its famous landmarks to its darkened
back streets, exploring the culture, history, and most
importantly the people that make it the great city it is
today. From the exiled writer recalling his appetite for
a lost lover, to the mad, homeless man directing traffic
in a freelance capacity... the contrasting perspectives of
these stories surprise and delight in equal measure, and
together present a new kind of guide to the city.

www.commapress.co.uk